This book is dedicated to all always raining where they are.

Remember there's a rainbow not far away.

This book is a work of fiction. Unless otherwise indicated all the names, characters, businesses, places, events in this book are either the product of the authors imagination or used in a fictitious manner. Any resemblance to actual persons living or dead or actual events is purely coincidental.

The book covers a period of modern history where there has been much change in the global approach to diversity. Non-diverse stereotypes are covered in the story and do not reflect the views of the author.

The copywrite of this book is owned by Ian Broadbent 2025

Ianbroadbentbooks.com

Foreword   December 2022 Preston Lancashire

The Christmas party season was in full swing, well as full swing as things got these days. In the years Colin had been in the pub and club game things had changed dramatically, this part of town once vibrant on a Saturday evening was now full of empty buildings and those that survived really had to carve out their own niche just to make ends meet. Retail stores had also abandoned the city centre for concrete out of town shopping parks taking the heart and soul with them. There had been a brief upsurge after the global pandemic but the town had found its level again, yep for Colin it would always be "Town" despite being given city status in the 2002 Queens Jubilee.

His latest venture was a retro bar in a long since converted bank and the formula was pretty simple. Lots of music from the 80's and 90's, reasonably priced drinks and not too much light and some very questionable dancing. In the good old days Colin had owned five pubs in this area but like many people had diversified, but this is where his heart really was, his old stomping ground and he had plans to make the city centre great again.

On the face of it he had done very well for himself, leaving school with few O levels and not attending college, a quiet guy who didn't give too much away and could be hard to read, not a person you would call a close friend but someone who would always be there for you and a sort of fixer who could help you out of all sorts of scrapes. Behind the cool façade the reality was his brain was always working at 100mph the proverbial duck with its legs paddling away under the water.

Everyone coming into the bar this Saturday night complained about the cold with the temperatures being below freezing for ten consecutive days. His bar manager Tracy muttered under her breath about yet another leering male customer who made some remark along the lines of "warm me up love", did every December not used to be this cold when she was young? It was only recent years where the weather didn't know if it was coming and going. To be fair it was cold, looking out on to Church Street Colin could see people's breath as they hailed taxi's or shouted at each other as they started to head home.

Colin remembered Christmas's in the past when he was a mere punter, when you had to queue to get into every venue and even needed tickets for special events. He was starting to sound like his dad he thought to himself, life moved on and in truth there were aspects of that trade he didn't miss. With other business interests he was comfortably off and unlike many of his customers he didn't have to worry about the cost of living.

He was brought back to earth when the alarm sounded as the rear exit alarm activated, the alarm and push bar had been fitted to stop customers using the emergency exit as a short cut through to the back alley and taxi rank, but in reality it hadn't reduced the route being used. He walked through to the back and saw the door hanging open, suddenly he heard a noise to his right and then a blow to the head as he was pulled into his own office. The last thing Colin remembered seeing was the room starting to spin and then a familiar voice said "and then there were two" then a prick to his arm then darkness.

Chapter One   October 1984 Leyland Lancashire

The five 14-year-old lads had been on one of their Saturday trips, they all went to a local comprehensive and lived for their Saturday afternoons. In the winter it was football and in the summer cricket but most of all the risk, excitement and camaraderie of a day out together. Normally this meant jumping on a train towards Manchester from Leyland as they were doing now. The station was on its knees, the whole area was having a hard time and Thatcher's promise of boom boom boom hadn't arrived just yet. The town was still dominated by the local vehicle industry, there were rumours that the government would take on the unions here too as had happened just down the road with the miners, short days were already underway as the building of cars, lorries and buses struggled against cheaper imports from open markets.

The town itself had little for teenagers, a snooker hall and a couple of youth clubs as the lads still weren't at pub age. The local factories still provided the majority of employment for Leyland with the traditional wake's weeks taking place each July turning the area in to a ghost town and in reality if you didn't work for British Leyland there was a good chance that you worked somewhere that supported the dominant employer.

But Colin, John, Pete, Dave and Chris never let any of this get them down, the railway gave them easy adventures with Blackpool to the North and West and Manchester and Liverpool to the south, they had even talked about a trip to London to follow their local football team after all the smoke and those strange cockney folk were only three hours away. As well as their sense of adventure their other common ethos was work meant play, all of them had part time work in local shops, farms and paper rounds giving them a few quid in their pocket to spend at weekends . No-one really knew where they went at weekends, parents would probably have said no, and other friends wouldn't have shared the same sense of adventure.

John tended to be the transport organiser, once they decided "where" he would come up with the "how". Normally the plan for the following weekend was hatched outside the chip shop on a Monday school lunchtime, by Thursday the route, time and plan were agreed and they would normally congregate on the platform ten minutes before the train was due.

This particular Saturday they had decided on Manchester, only 45 minutes direct by train and they were gambling on not paying the fare. It was possible to board the train easily enough at Leyland and the ticket office was often closed anyway. Cutbacks meant there were few staff on the train and they knew how to sneak out of Manchester Victoria station without passing the ticket collectors. The saving they made contributed to whatever activities they had planned.

Chris normally decided on the "what" and today they would go to watch Manchester City play Arsenal. This was years before the advent of the Premier League but the excitement amongst the lads was palpable. What would the score be, who would be playing and would there be fighting in or around the stadium. None of them supported either team but the adrenalin of being part of a big crowd, the reek of alcohol, witty comments, crude songs and the smell of cigarettes, as Pete had commented previously it was like "the smell of football".

There was no sign of the train, the dirty local commuter trains were well past their sell by date and frequently broke down, the only way of knowing if this was the case would be the ringing of the station phone and shortly after, if the ticket office was open, someone would come out and shout from the bridge that the train was late. Today though they spotted the train motoring towards them from Preston, smoke billowing from its engines, the train was coming – the day was on.

Salford came into view followed by Manchester city centre, the view on the final run in to Manchester was like a Lowry painting, whilst there was rumour and news about reinventing Manchester City Centre it still looked a long way off in 1984. Victoria station had lost a lot of its grand façade, once a destination in its own right it now only served local commuter routes around the northwest.

Before the game they visited the city centre and the big stores before dining on a takeaway of chips, scraps and gravy, scraps being the bits of batter that fell off the fried fish. A coach out to the stadium followed where they arrived an hour before the game was due to start and before they knew it, they were on their way home. The journey home started with bypassing the ticket barrier at Victoria station before boarding the train, it was a cold Autumn evening and soon dark. The train rattled along through Bolton and Chorley before joining the main line close to Leyland, as it did John commented that it seemed to be going much faster than usual and lurched across the points before speeding through Leyland where they were supposed to alight. Whilst his mates labelled him a travel geek for commenting, a look of panic set in on all their faces when they realised the train wasn't going to stop as they had all promised to be home around 7pm making up various excuses as to where they had been for the day. Other passengers sat with puzzled looks on their faces as to why the train had not stopped, what they did not know at this stage was the train had passed a signal at danger and was about to pass two more. The driver realising that the engine wasn't responding to a brake application warned the passengers in the leading carriage to move to the rear one as a collision was imminent. What they also didn't realise was that the driver had a passenger in his cab who he had been talking to on the journey from Manchester distracting him from his duties, this meant there was no vacuum in the brake system when the braking application was made, what was about to ensue was totally avoidable.

The train thundered through Preston station its horn blowing with startled passengers on the platform moving away from the edge, the passengers on the train were in panic mode as they tried to get out of the front carriage. The five lads were some of the last out of the front carriage and as the train collided with a stationery engine just north of the station Dave was on the joining footplate between the two carriages, and suddenly everything went black.

Chapter 2   October 1988 Preston

Chris, John, Colin and Pete were on the Thursday 7.30am train into Preston from Leyland, after leaving school the friendship hadn't diminished despite them now pursuing their different lives. The train had a mix of workers commuting in to "town" and 6th formers with pre college activities and arrived in Preston just 5 minutes after leaving Leyland.

It hadn't gone unnoticed it was four years to the day since that fateful trip to Manchester when the train crashed and derailed on the way home. Whilst the four of them had survived pretty much unscathed Dave had not been so lucky. His body trapped between the concertinaed train it had taken 6 hours to release, partly due to the location of the incident and partly due to the force of impact, whilst Dave had survived the accident, he lost both legs and suffered other significant injuries. With the compensation paid to them in settlement from British Rail, Dave's family had started a new life in the Shetland Islands breeding sheep and ponies. This had made regular contact difficult, and they had only travelled once as a group to see him since, that in itself had been a difficult journey to what John had described as a Godforsaken outpost.

As they exited Preston station, they all touched the plaque in memory of the 1984 accident, whilst they had survived and Dave lived on three people had lost their lives, whilst the drivers actions had saved many more he was ultimately found negligent for the accident. They went their separate ways agreeing to meet at 6pm at the Old Bull pub to raise a glass for Dave and exorcise the ghosts that still danced in front of them from that day in October 1984.

Colin headed up Church Street and the ten-minute walk to the bank where he worked, sports journalism had been his first choice but he had ended up working on a training scheme at the local authority before being snapped up as part of a banks recruitment drive a few months later. He hated Thursdays, as it was the traditional pay day the bank would be queued out of the door for most of the day as people rushed in to draw out their weekly pay, in addition it was their late night opening so it meant he would be the last to join the guys for beers at the old bull, mind you he would soon neck a few down to catch up.

At lunch time he wandered down Church Street window shopping before buying a particularly unhealthy lunch on the basis of lining his stomach for the evening. The afternoon was busier than usual, he smiled to himself when one customer who had drawn out £90 out of his £100 weekly pay check earlier returned for the remaining £10, after paying his mum weekly board the rest was clearly invested in local betting shops. The good thing about being busy was the afternoon passed really quickly and before he knew it, he was walking down Church Street to meet the others. The Old Bull was a traditional pub with a lounge and snug and a regular venue for live music, as he opened the door the jukebox blared out and a wall of cigarette smoke hit him, but he could see the others deep in conversation at the rear.

Being reasonably local and seemingly reliable Colin had been given the responsibility of taking "half" the front door key to the Bank home with him, he laughed to himself thinking about the managers last words from the manager "Colin don't forget you have one half of the door key, don't be late tomorrow and don't drink too much tonight". As part of the security measures for opening the branch there were two keyholders who each had half the key which fitted together and then opened the front door meaning no one person could open the branch on their own. The process involved the two staff meeting at an arranged point, opening the bank and checking inside before signalling to the remaining staff it was safe to enter. He really wasn't sure whether he was deemed reliable, local or just a big lad or maybe a combination of the three. Maybe he was just seen as a good prospect, a new starter had twice accidently pulled out "the magic fiver" from the till which automatically called the Police, and it was Colin who had been entrusted with delivering the additional training to make sure it didn't happen again. The first time it had taken the Police 7 minutes to attend but the second time, over 15 minutes, the theory being the more false alarms the slower the response.

Anyway, he sincerely hoped the alarm didn't go off tonight, he was looking forward to meeting the lads and he would take some tracking down if there was an issue. He joined the rest of the guys, and the first pint of Boddingtons disappeared in less than 5 minutes. He batted away the normal banter from the rest of the gang, this was pretty standard stuff and related to his salary and the fact that they presumed he had access to the safe.

The night wore on and they visited the Black Horse, Louis Long Bar and then tried their luck with the ladies in Yates Wine Lodge. But with the words of his manager ringing in his ears still Colin decided to head home catching the 111 bus which took longer than the train but when you had had a few drinks was a lot closer door to door. Before he left though he was convinced to have one more for the road, it had been a great night reminiscing even if his suggestion to go and visit Dave in the Shetlands had met a mixed response. It's alright for you said the others with your salary and access to the safe, it's a lot of money to visit that shithole. What if I did have access to the safe? Colin asked his friends, but before they could answer he had slipped out of the wine lodge to catch the bus home and before the next stop he was already fast asleep.

Chapter 3   November 1990 South London

After College and University Pete had moved to London and was desperate to further his political ambitions, he knew this could take many years, but he would prepare by volunteering where he could in the hope that he could secure a researchers post in the Conservative Party. Not many people at school had shown an interest in politics and certainly not the Tories but with family history at a local level it was where his heart lay. For now, he was living in New Cross in a pretty grim bedsit that was costing him £50 per week. The street where he lived had been grand in its day he supposed, but now the three storey town houses were split into multiple bedsits with transient lodgers who came and went like the weather. Nights could be noisy though with residents playing loud music and parties springing up, especially in the summer months. Whilst most people lived side by side without problems, racial tensions could be high and after all it was less than 10 years some of the worst riots seen on UK streets. just down the road in Brixton and surrounding areas.

The local high street was a mix of takeaways, mini markets and beauty salons, the diverse mix of residents created a myriad of stores to supply their tastes and Pete loved it, it was exactly why he moved to the capital to experience new cultures and ideas. Travel was also so much easier, he had already visited Paris and

Amsterdam by train and ferry taking the boat train from London Victoria Station, he had also read about the plans to open a tunnel between the UK and Europe with direct trains taking you to Europe in a couple of hours, he couldn't wait for this to happen.
Pete worked out every day keeping himself very fit and always dressed very stylishly, during his teens he had suffered with acne but now had a smooth complexion, always tanned and turned heads wherever he went. Most days started with a 5-6 mile run normally over towards the open area of Blackheath or Greenwich Park then evenings normally involved working out at the local gym unless work got in the way.

In his free time, he either spent the time on his political research or walked the streets of London, he loved the buzz of famous landmark streets but equally the wide open spaces such as Hyde Park and the various heaths. He would never forget his upbringing and where he came from, but Pete knew then that he would never live in Leyland again. He still saw John, Chris and Colin in his regular trips home, and they would sometimes visit him too sleeping on the floor after late nights then the night bus home. But whilst he hadn't shared with them his political ambition, for fear of ridicule, he also hadn't shared his other secret, one that he was sure would be harder to accept by his mates. He didn't enjoy lying but equally it was a hassle he didn't need right now so he sort of ignored the problem.

Today he was working at the Royal Standard Public House in Greenwich, they paid well and he liked the clientele, they were "his sort" and generally well read and he enjoyed debating with some of the customers on his afternoon shifts. Once he had finished he was heading up to a casino in Soho where he would again work on the bar, he didn't enjoy this as much as the customers were normally drunk or arrogant or both, but again it paid well and meant he could visit some of his favourite haunts before and after his shifts. He also made a fortune in tips with his easy-going friendly personality, whilst softly spoken his voice gave off a friendly but confident air that people warmed to. This evening unexpectedly one of the customers had come on to him leaving Pete under no illusion that it could be a very lucky night indeed, certainly not one of the regulars but a familiarity that Pete couldn't quite put his finger on, anyway life was too short to worry and he was determined to enjoy the evening.

Next morning he looked over at the guy in bed next to him before thinking to himself how happy he could finally be himself. He had no idea how long he lay there in and out of sleep but was woken by the loud ringing of the payphone in the corridor of the house the bedsit was in, as the nearest to the phone he had often answered the phone but had now told those close to him to let the phone ring twice then ring again, this is exactly what had happened on this occasion. It was his Mum excitedly asking if he had seen the news, what did he think and did this change things? As he hung up and wandered back to his room it was a question, he asked himself, Maggie Thatcher had been PM for 11 years but now she was gone, what did this mean for him – he wasn't sure.

He returned to the tiny kitchen and put the kettle on, embarrassingly he couldn't even remember his new companions name so he gambled and made both a tea and a coffee and returned to the bedroom and climbed back under the sheets Pete turned on the TV and watched the coverage of Thatcher leaving office, whilst his family were staunch conservative voters he felt she had lost her way in recent years and like many leaders had outstayed her welcome. The last few months had seen plotting from the benches and whilst he had thought she would ride out the storm it wasn't to be, but who would emerge as the next leader? Many of the potentials hadn't covered themselves with glory in the way they had plotted generally with personal rather than broader aims.

London itself had been a battleground with the 1990 Poll Tax riots, thousands of people had come together for peaceful protest against this Thatcher initiative but as the day wore on the demonstrations had become more and more violent and in the end there were running battles on Whitehall and the surrounding streets, Pete himself had headed up to Trafalgar Square but on exiting the tube at Charing Cross was shocked at the level of destruction and pure hatred of those still "protesting".

His new friend sleepily leant across and started stroking him whilst the coverage unfolded on TV. Mrs Thatcher had left Downing Street for the last time with her husband Dennis and was speaking to the nation, Pete could never understand why those leaving office had this chance to speak and try and justify everything they had done but supposed that after 11 years it wasn't a lot to ask. The TV cameras showed Dennis holding the car door for her and as she climbed in there was a flashing of light as the newspaper cameras tried to get their shots, as they did it he had a flashback to the previous evening and where they had met and suddenly he realised who was sharing his bed

Chapter 4   November 1988 Bressay Shetlands

Dave watched the ferry leave Lerwick down Bressay Sound and towards the North Sea, it was a relatively calm early evening and the passengers looked sure to have a steady crossing down to Orkney then onwards to Aberdeen on the overnight ferry, he had joked with his Dad that you could fly to Australia in the time it took to get back to Lancashire from here with the ferry alone taking 13 hours to Aberdeen.

The Shetlands sat to the Northeast of Scotland and they had settled on Bressay one of the smaller islands opposite the islands "capital" of Lerwick. There wasn't much on the island, a school, post office/shop, pub, several farms and a few guest houses mainly there for the bird watchers and walkers who visited in the summer months. The population on Bressay was around 300 people and reducing year on year, most of the youths he had met around his age left for university and only came back to visit. There was a small car ferry that made the 5-minute crossing each hour between Bressay and Lerwick also bringing vital supplies and the visitors. During the summer the population could literally double as tourists came to discover nature and the locals cashed in selling locally made produce or hiring out the famous Shetland ponies for people to ride.

During the longest days of May and June it was literally

light for 20 hours a day given how far north they were, but even then, the temperature rarely reached much more than 15 Celsius. In the winter months daylight was restricted to around 5-6 hours and although they often missed the bitterly cold weather in the gulf stream it was more often than not wet, grey and windy. His sister helped in the one pub on the island and in the summer mainly served tourists keen to sample "the real Shetlands" but in winter there was a darker side as many of the locals turned to the bottle to cope with the loneliness and grey weather. Sharon had been an absolute rock for him, following that fateful night she had dressed him, bathed him, consoled him and on one occasion found him when he had considered ending it all. Although she hadn't been on the train that night she had suffered almost as much as him being uprooted from all her friends and cut off on this wild island, but he had never heard her complain. Whilst he had understood the compensation, they received following the accident was substantial he sometimes thought his parents had used it to fund their dream of farming sheep and ponies up here on Bressay.

He wheeled himself down to the lighthouse most nights, there were only really three roads on the island and this one stretched from their farmhouse by the little ferry terminal down to the light. He would watch the nightly ferry leave for the mainland until the lights disappeared into the distance and then generally visit Gerry the lighthouse keeper. Gerry was paid to maintain the light to ensure it was switched on and off as well as maintaining the foghorn for when the weather wasn't clear, he and his wife took in guests as well in the summer months but had actually relocated here from the Midlands in the 1970's when city life became too much. Gerry was convinced that Trinity House that ran all the lighthouses round the UK would soon want him gone as an automation programme was put into place. He used to rant about this and couldn't understand how this could all possibly be controlled remotely, nor what would happen if something broke down.

The lighthouse was a collection of low buildings full of all sorts of redundant equipment then obviously the light tower itself. It could be a little creepy but certainly a great place if you wanted to disappear from the world, a mile from the nearest property and only a local farmer occasionally passing to tend to his sheep. Indeed, many of the visitors who stayed in the summer months came to escape their day to day world.

Normally, once he had chatted with Gerry, he would wheel himself the 3 miles back home, the lane was just about wide enough so a car could pass him but in the winter the traffic was very light and most nights he didn't see anyone at all. His sister nagged him about being out on his own, what if something happened, who would know where you are? She used to say. Working in the pub she also knew the island residents who tended to drink more than they should before driving home.

There was no chance of being caught drink driving here as the Police were based on the main island in Lerwick, on the rare occasion they did come over the master of the little car ferry would radio ahead to warn everyone that they were on their way over. In fact a few days before she had joked with Dave that even if he did get a lift from someone there was a good chance the driver would have been drinking, equally his wheelchair could be hit by a drink driver so he may as well have a few drinks with Gerry then wheel himself back.

He wanted to be back at a reasonable hour this evening as tomorrow he had to visit the physio over in Lerwick, although a short journey, being very independent it meant getting himself down to the ferry for the short crossing then pulling himself up the hill to the clinic in the main town. Whilst there he would shop for some supplies and have a drink with friends he had made before reversing the journey in the afternoon. Dave grimaced to himself, the trip across to Lerwick was a big effort, he had dreamed about exploring the world but now he had to wait for the world to come to him and it didn't come very often.

It had been a surprise when his old friend Colin had said he was making the journey up to see him, he knew what a tricky journey it was taking the overnight sleeper train up to Aberdeen then the ferry across. Although they had been a wider group of friends, he and Colin were particularly close and had been able to talk to each other about absolutely anything. Despite everything that happened and the distance since the accident there was no awkwardness and they had spent a great three days catching up, swapping stories and drinking. Colin was doing ok working in the bank in Preston but deep-down Dave knew that this wouldn't be a long term role. Colin had itchy feet and an arrogance about him that told people he thought he belonged in a different place.

As much as Dave thought he knew Colin well he had still been amazed by the plan he had presented him with. If it had been anyone else, he might have thought it was a joke but he knew Colin was a serious thinker and every inch of what he had shared with Dave had been meticulously researched. On their last day together Colin had asked Dave if he was willing to join him with the plan but Dave had said he needed time to reflect, Colin had left for Lerwick and the ferry home that night and said that was fine but he wanted an answer before he left the Shetlands.

So as Dave watched the ferry pass, he strained his eyes to see Colin but the fading light and distance made it impossible although he convinced himself that he recognised the person stood alone at the stern.

Gerry was up at the top of the lighthouse making sure everything was operating as it should and watched Dave watching the ferry pass, he knew as soon as it was out of sight that Dave would come in for a wee dram or a longer drink. As Gerry turned away a flash of light caught his eye and he saw Dave flash a light towards the ferry several times, he couldn't understand why Dave would do this and was even more surprised to see a light flash back three times from the back of the ferry too. As he made his way downstairs something in his mind told Gerry not to mention anything to Dave and to instead reflect and try and reason what he had just witnessed.

Chapter 5   November 1988 Morecambe Bay Lancs

John stood on the beach at Glasson Dock, or Glasson as it was known to locals looking out across Morecambe Bay and the Irish Sea. Since starting his apprenticeship on Sealink ferries he had moved the 20 miles north from Leyland to be closer to Heysham where he worked on the daily ferry service across to Belfast. He worked 4 days on and 4 days off so when he wasn't working, he tended to walk along the beaches close to where he lived or watch the occasional visiting coasters load and unload in Glasson Dock.

In the 18th century the Port of Lancaster had decided to build a dock at Glasson because of the difficulties of navigating up the River Lune to the port at Lancaster and at one time Glasson had been able to accommodate 25 merchant ships. In the 19th century the port had been connected to the canal network and cargo could come through Glasson and onwards to the mill towns of the Northwest and beyond, there had even been a busy shipyard primarily repairing but also building small ships.

When the railways came a little branch line connected Glasson to Lancaster, but passenger and goods services had ended many years before. Despite this a limited amount of commercial traffic still used the dock, with outbound shipments including coal for the Isle of Man and Scotland and incoming cargoes included animal foodstuffs and fertilizer.

John had a deep fascination with the sea and had long been planning a career on the seas, a less than spectacular set of exam results meant that he was doing it the hard way as an apprentice cook on the daily ferry service that linked Northern Ireland with the North West of England, there were rumours the service wouldn't last much longer but for now he was happy to have one step on the ladder and when he was on board but off shift he would spend his spare time watching his elder colleagues at work gathering as much knowledge as possible from them. There were some rough crossings on the 6-hour journey but John was born with sea legs and he took a grim pleasure in seeing others struggle in the choppy conditions. Primarily the ferry carried unaccompanied HGV trailers, and it would take around 4-5 hours to load each day and in addition there would be up to 20 accompanied trailers with the drivers also joining the ferry for the crossing. Heysham was quite a small port with sailings to the Isle of Man, Southern and Northern Ireland and occasionally the military would use the port to transfer equipment over to Northern Ireland out of the sight of the larger ports.

His small flat in Glasson was above the 18th century Dalton Arms directly overlooking the harbour and the small array of cafes, shops and the post office which served the 500 locals and visitors from all over the

Northwest. From here he cycled to Heysham for his shifts in all-weather with the 12 miles taking him 45 minutes each way subsequently he was lean and fit with all the money he saved put towards his studies for the qualification he would need to make his dream job of ships master. John came from an Irish Catholic family from the west coast of Ireland close to Cobh and it was his grandparents tales of a life at sea that had started his own fascination, his Grandad claiming to have helped row passengers out to the Titanic on its final voyage as it made its final call before heading in to the Atlantic. But each time he told the stories the adventures seemed to get more spectacular and less believable but even, so he loved to hear what the old sea dog had to say.

John had spent almost all of his childhood in Leyland where his parents had moved in the early 1970's, his dad worked at the local rubber factory whilst his Mum had mainly stayed at home doing part time work in the evenings as was quite common at the time. They were both staunch republicans with very strong views and John always found it puzzling that they had chosen to settle in England, however they had never forced those views on him and had supported him as he grew up, he had no complaints. He had one older brother who had rebelled in his teens and left home whilst John was still 9, there had been very little contact with him since and no one in the family really spoke about where he was. Every time John tried to start a conversation it was quickly shut down which he found frustrating, up until him leaving John had looked up to his older brother and looked back fondly at the times Kieran had spent kicking the ball with him in the back garden or on the local school playing field.

After John had left, his parents had taken in regular lodgers, they would arrive almost without warning and stay for 3-4 months rarely leaving the house then leave and never return. His Mum said it helped with the family income, but he was never sure how these people afforded to stay with the family as they didn't seem to work.

Although he wasn't far from "home" the shifts and geography made it hard to return home regularly, he missed his friends and in particular Pete, Colin, Dave and Chris, he had only seen Dave once since he moved up to the Shetlands but spoke to Pete, Colin and Chris regularly. In fact, Colin had visited recently and they had a night out in Lancaster where they had both drunk far too much before sharing a taxi back to Glasson. John always considered Colin to be a bit of a fantasist and was surprised he had taken a job in retail banking, with his quick brain and ability to charm almost anyone he would be a perfect entrepreneur with his crazy schemes, whilst the latest plan from Colin had been the craziest yet, John had no doubt that Colin was serious and was able to make it come true.

John, however, had wanted no part in it, he didn't want anything to come between him and his career at sea so had given a firm no way mate as they had parted the next day. For a split second John had seen a fiery look in Colin's eye before he turned and left for the bus to Lancaster then the train home and knew he had upset Colin, but they weren't kids any more he had his own life now and couldn't be expected to join in everything the gang had planned. After all Dave was in Shetlands, Pete planned to move to London and he himself no longer lived in Leyland.

John spotted the Isle of Man ferry in the distance making its way through the tidal areas of Morecambe Bay and in to Heysham on its morning crossing from the Island. The King Orry was the island lifeline and as well as its load of passengers travelling to the mainland would have empty trailers ready to be replaced by produce on the return journey to fill the shelves of the shops on the Island. Although less than a four-hour crossing the route was notoriously difficult as it approached the mainland with narrow channels and fast moving tides. Heysham harbour itself had a very narrow entrance and with strong cross winds could be a difficult port to dock in, it needed dredging regularly and at certain lower tides larger vessels had to anchor in the bay and wait for the tide to rise. A few masters had blots on their careers misjudging the conditions and he knew if he was to make his dream job come true, he would have a lot to learn.

Today though the conditions were about average, the King Orry approached without missing a beat and soon disappeared around the headland as it made its final approach towards Heysham. John was on the nightshift but would first try and catch a few hours' sleep, Mondays were one of his favourite days as the Landlord of the Dalton Arms went fishing with a friend and his wife Heather would come and spend the afternoon with him, these afternoons had been initiated by Heather herself who sought solace from her husband who often drank too much when working behind the bar and then got aggressive when he headed upstairs to bed. Several months ago he had heard shouting then as he had got up for water in the night and he had found Heather crying in the kitchen, after consoling her things had progressed quickly and they often spent several afternoons together when shifts allowed, she was 10 years older than him, experienced but didn't want anything from him other than his time, ear and well the other thing as well. Today after they had made love, he must have drifted off to sleep and when he woke he was surprised to hear the windows rattling as the easterly wind had picked up and a storm was brewing.

He watched Heather as she slept for several minutes before tenderly waking her touching her naked body and tickling here where he knew it would have the maximum affect. He whispered in her ear that he would have to head to Heysham for the night crossing and she would have to get the bar ready for the evening opening hours, he watched her slim body tease him as she returned to her own room in her nightie and then he showered and got his uniform ready for tonight's crossing. Glasson was a bit of a one-horse town and as he got on his bike there were few people around, not helped as the weather seemed to be moving in quickly. Heather shouted from the back of the pub "Good luck Sailor" as he quickly picked up speed on his bike, normally on the ride to Heysham on a Monday his mind would be full of thoughts of the time he had spent with Heather but tonight he couldn't shift the image of fire in Colin's eyes when he had said no to him, they had been friends for 12 years and he had never seen that look before, it made him even more certain that Colin's latest crazy idea was already on the drawing board and that he had taken for granted that John would be in on the scheme. Should he reconsider? As he headed north, and the rain started to pour his mood darkened like the black clouds on this stormy November evening.

Chapter 6   December 1988 Londonderry

Around 200 miles to the west of Glasson Dock Chris was based in Londonderry, a member of the Queen's Lancashire Regiment (QLR) which was an infantry regiment of the British Army and part of the Kings Division which had been formed in 1970 through the amalgamation of two other infantry regiments. As a regiment they had significant experience in Northern Ireland with around 10 different operations in the 70's and 80's and had also served in the Falklands after the war in the South Atlantic as well as several tours in divided Germany. They were headquartered at Fulwood Barracks in Preston with territorial units based around the Northwest.

Derry (officially Londonderry) is the second largest city in Northern Island with the old walled city lying on the banks of the River Foyle. The population of this ancient city was around 80,000 with its position as a seaport and proximity to the border with County Donegal and Southern Island ensuring it was a prominent trading post. The city had deteriorated after the second world war, with unemployment and development stagnating. It had become a focal point for the civil rights movement in Northern Ireland after Catholics were discriminated against under Unionist government in Northern Ireland, both politically and economically.

Throughout that period the most serious charge against the Northern Ireland government was not that it had been directly responsible for widespread discrimination, but that it allowed discrimination on such a scale over a substantial segment of Northern Ireland. A Civil rights demonstration in 1968 was banned by the Government and blocked with force by the Royal Ulster Constabulary and as things escalated over the following year the August 1969 parades started events which became known as the battle of the Bogside when Catholic rioters fought with the Police leading to wider civil disorder across Northern Ireland which was often pinpointed as the starting point of "the troubles"
A few years later on Sunday 30 January 1972, 13 unarmed civilians were shot dead by British paratroopers during a civil rights march in the bogside area with another 13 wounded and one man later dying of his wounds. This event came to be known around the world as bloody Sunday.

Chris had completed his training with the Queens Lancashire Regiment earlier in the year but as he had only just passed his 18th birthday this was his first tour of duty with the Regiment. He loved the camaraderie of his fellow soldiers who were mainly drawn from the North West of England, but as someone who loved to explore he hated the fact that when off duty they were pretty much confined to the barracks on the outskirts of Londonderry, things were extremely tense and it simply wasn't safe to walk the streets or use public transport, there was no hiding place for a young squaddie.

The Irish Republican Army (IRA) were currently stronger than at any point during "the troubles". The security services had found them almost impossible to penetrate over the last twelve months and as a result the IRA's activity had been particularly deadly. They had become by far the most active of republican paramilitary groups and certainly now saw itself as the army of an all-island republic and were designated as a terrorist organisation in the United Kingdom and an unlawful organisation in the Republic of Ireland – both of whose authority it rejected. Their aim was simple, a united reunified Ireland and currently all sides were at stalemate.

Although discrete discussions had taken place between the movements political wing, Sinn Fein, and the UK Government deadly attacks were still a regular reality, whilst their most high profile action of the 1980's had involved an assassination attempt in Brighton on Margaret Thatcher at the Conservative party annual conference killing and wounding members of parliament, attacks on the British army who they saw as legitimate targets continued regularly.

1988 had been a particularly bloody year for both sides of the ongoing conflict, in March an elite SAS team of the British Army had shot dead an IRA active unit in Gibraltar and only a week later mourners at the funeral of those shot dead were targeted by a terrorist group who considered themselves loyal to the UK. Two days later two British army corporals were abducted, beaten and shot dead after accidentally driving in to the funeral cortege of those targeted at the aforementioned funeral.

The killings had continued throughout the summer with over 30 British soldiers dying in various attacks across Northern Ireland. Things were out of control, something needed to change.

Chris was not a fool, he realised that life in the Army would not be just like the posters in the recruitment office in Preston Town Centre, his family followed the news avidly and his father in particular had been proud when he said he was heading over the water with the Queens Lancashire Regiment. He had joined late in 1987 and completed the basic 6-month training and after a short leave period had gone on to a further 6 months training on his chosen trade of logistical support. The posting to Londonderry had been not long after this and fortunately he had managed to spend an evening in Preston with Colin, John and Pete before the regiment tour, which was due to last 6 months. He had always dreamed of joining the Army and he had been massively proud when his family had watched him pass out and become a fully-fledged soldier at the barracks just a few months ago. As part of his logistical learning, he had reported back earlier than some of his regiment to begin the preparation involved in moving a full regiment across the North sea and in to the base at Londonderry.

Tonight, they were patrolling in an armoured Land Rover Defender, their role was defensive, mainly observational and not offensive but at the briefings they had attended daily since arriving in the city he knew it was only a matter of time before he would be involved in a full on firefight. The thought neither excited or worried him although as they crossed into the bogside he did give a thought to his Mum who he knew would be worried sick about him and would be glued to the BBC news each evening watching for news of any attacks or action in Northern Ireland. The damp grey day had given way to a cold night with clear skies lit quite vividly by the almost full moon, the streets were quiet which wasn't always a good sign, the local community tended to retreat behind their front doors when they knew something was about to go down, although the media often showed images of the patrols being stoned and abuse shouted at by youngsters, particularly on summer nights, it was the nights when no one was on the street that put everyone on the highest of alerts.

He had tried to call his girlfriend Jackie earlier, she was two years older than him and had left home for university and was becoming harder and harder to speak to, the final straw seemed to be when he finally admitted that he would not be home for Christmas. He had expected this somewhat as she had always described him as her bit of rough and he had convinced himself she would find someone who stimulated her mind more amongst the academics at university. Her family ironically had emigrated from Ireland to the UK some years ago settling in Liverpool initially before moving to central Lancashire when the house building boom of the 1980's started. Chris wasn't hugely upset that things maybe wouldn't work out, he just felt that he deserved to be told so he made a pledge to write to her when their patrol was finished for the evening. Earlier in the evening, unknown to the patrol and indeed the British Army, a chip shop owner had reported to the Royal Ulster Constabulary (RUC) that a customer had dropped a piece of paper in his shop, the paper appeared to show the names and address of a family who were likely to be targeted on the local Creggan estate in Derry. This tactic had been used in other areas of Northern Ireland with bombs detonated when the RUC arrived at the address to investigate so the officer who took the call decided to escalate the issue rather than warn RUC colleagues or pass through channels to the Security Services.

Creggan was a passionately republican area of Derry and as the patrol entered the area the vigilance levels increased another notch. Chris was sat in the passenger seat in the front with his eyes firmly focussed on the areas to the left as they entered Inniscarn Road. As they made the left turn into the 1950's built street a huge explosion ripped through a property on the opposite side of the road, the shock lifted the Landover from the road and for Chris the world seemed to go in to slow motion. As the defender landed with a bang on its wheels his Sergeant and regiment colleagues in the back started to scream instructions and record verbally what they were seeing. Despite all his training and the orders being screamed at him by his sergeant, Chris opened the door of the Landover and ran towards the burning house entering through the space where the door had stood, as he did this his comrades in the Landover realised they were now under sustained fire.

Chapter 7   December 1988 Preston Lancashire

Colin walked up Church Street in Preston listening to his Walkman and his beloved latest U2 album, it was almost Christmas and later in the day this main shopping area would be full of shoppers ensuring they had all their gifts purchased in time for Christmas. But at 8:15am it was just the normal workers heading in to complete another shift wherever they worked. It was almost the shortest day of the year and therefore was only just starting to get fully light, whilst there had been colder days the light rain just seemed to add to the cold so the chill went through to the bones. Although many of the buildings had impressive facades the street lights and rain together accentuated the colour of the stone which just added to the greyness of the day. Colin stopped off at the small newsagents on Church Street to buy his normal morning newspaper before continuing the walk up the slight incline of Church Street where he reached the meeting point as a keyholder at 8:20am.

The procedure at the bank was simple, they both had half a key each for the safe and both had a front door key meaning that even if someone was lying in wait for whoever entered they wouldn't have access to the safe. On this morning it should be the assistant manager Kevin who went forward opened the door and silenced the alarm carrying out a cursory check of the interior to make sure there was no sign of suspicious activity. Colin waited for 5 minutes for Kevin to arrive at the meeting point and was just starting to think he wasn't going to arrive when he saw the front door to the bank open slightly and Kevin waved Colin forward. Whilst this wasn't in line with company procedure it wasn't the first time Kevin had gone in early normally making sure the kettle was on for when the rest of the 25 staff arrived for their morning tea and coffee. Really, he was supposed to wait for the second keyholder to arrive before carrying out the check then signal with a raised hand if all was clear or with a hand on the forehead if the 2nd keyholder wasn't to proceed. As long as all was clear the 2nd keyholder then had the job of letting the other staff in as they arrived between 8.30am and 9am using the spyhole in the door to check their validity with the first keyholder then ensuring the safe was open and the tills could be signed out to the tellers ready for the day.

Today promised to be a busy day as the biggest employer locally Leyland Motors were due to pay their staff, for 6 months an industrial dispute had been taking place with workers seeking improved pay and conditions. The town had regularly featured on the local and national news and some commentators said that if it wasn't resolved soon the death bell for the company would start to toll. But both management and the unions had hammered out an agreement and as part of the agreement employees would receive a Christmas bonus. As part of their last stand the union had insisted this would be paid to employees in cash to avoid a delay in cashing the pay cheques so close to Christmas, in effect the employees were due to receive their weekly pay cheque then two times that value in cash, an unusual arrangement indeed that had caused concerns in the bank branch about the amount of cash they would need which had been a hot topic of discussion in the staff room for over a week now.

Colin walked the final few steps to the bank door and as it came ajar he saw Kevins face appear as usual, he didn't look himself with his face having a crumpled worried look and his eyes narrowed like he was in some sort of pain, Colin stepped forward and as he became level with the door a hand dragged him in and a masked gunman brandishing a shotgun threw him to the floor hitting his head on a pillar as he fell. As he recovered from the shock he looked over to Kevin and saw he was being held hands tied behind his back and blood running down the back of his neck, the guy holding him was holding a pistol to his neck.

Colin's assailant turned him on to his front removing the keys from his pockets and immediately ran towards the till area where the large walk in safe stood. The second member of the gang then spoke urgently but amazingly steadily to them both outlining what they both had to do next. He said that Kevins wife was being held elsewhere and made clear what the outcome would be if they didn't comply with instructions. It would turn out that in the middle of the previous night masked gunmen had held Kevin and his wife hostage and this morning five members of the gang had driven Kevin in to Preston in a van whilst the 6th member of the gang drove his wife in a car gagged and bound in the boot as the attempt to rob the bank unfolded. Kevin now had the sickening choice of either letting all the other employees enter their workplace in to a hostage situation or potentially see his loving wife come to harm if he made an attempt to raise the alarm to his colleagues.

Suddenly the bell to the front door rang followed by a loud knock, the first colleague had arrived. Open the fucking door and no one gets hurt said the gunman and Colin did as he was told, reached forward and opened the door slightly and as soon as his colleague entered she too was roughly pulled in to the building and forced to sit against the wall next to Kevin. This continued for the next 10 minutes at which point there were now 12 people sat with their backs against the wall in the main banking hall.

Another member of the gang worked quickly to blindfold and tie the hands of the bank colleagues when suddenly sirens were heard in the distance. They could be going anywhere shouted one gunman but the sirens certainly seemed to be getting closer thought Colin. The first member of the gang reiterated to them all that if everyone did as they were asked no-one would get hurt,

Colin kept his eyes to the ground, he couldn't bring himself to look at his colleagues who knew it was he that had been opening the door even though they knew he would have had little choice.

Unbeknown to them all inside the bank a cleaner at the large Marks and Spencer store across the road had been taking a break after starting their morning shift at 5am. He had seen two staff go in and then another seemed to stumble through the door as the door slammed shut behind them, there was no sign of the lights going on which was very odd given the dark damp day that it was so they he had called 999 suggesting that something unusual was going down at the largest bank in town. The emergency call handler was initially sceptical of the report and had asked for a lot of detail before passing the detail on to the Police and all the time the cleaner was away from the window and unable to see what else if anything was happening.

Things then just seemed to happen very quickly with another bank colleague ringing the bell and finding no-one came to the door and the first Police Rover patrol car screeched to a halt outside the bank. The arriving officer banged on the door and tried to peer through the frosted windows and receiving no reply escalated the emergency to his superior asking for a response unit and immediate back up. Just 5 minutes later back up arrived and the perimeter of the bank was sealed, with information from arriving bank colleagues they were able to deduce that there were at least 10 people in the bank presumably being held hostage. Whilst there had been no reports of gunshots and none of the witnesses had reported seeing anyone acting suspiciously an armed response unit was requested from the county headquarters and by 9.30am the bank was totally surrounded with Police also watching from neighbouring rooftops but there was no sign of any movement inside and phone calls remained unanswered.

A further call came in to the emergency room citing a Vauxhall Cavalier Saloon registered to an address in nearby Blackburn and belonging to a bank employee parked in a loading bay on the adjacent Avenham Street, when approached by shopworkers trying to receive an inward delivery muffled sounds and a slight rocking could be seen coming from the car. Two of the officers from the special response unit were despatched to the scene and were able to enter the vehicle quickly where Kevin's wife amazingly calmly told them how a gang had entered their house the night before, bound and gagged them before taking Kevin to the branch to presumably rob the contents.

The commander of the Police response operation attempted to make contact by phone and megaphone without success and an hour in to the incident a major crisis was unfolding. Preston had not seen anything like this before and the Police were having to hold back a growing number of onlookers. A decision was made to simultaneously enter the bank from the front and the yard at the back with armed and protected officers taking the lead. In full view of the watching public the rescue attempt commenced and within 5 minutes what appeared to be employees from the bank were being led out with their hands on their heads, they were put in to Police response vans and driven from the scene. The siege, as it was later to be known, seemed to be coming to an end with staff being released without harm.

The Lancashire Evening Post was a provincial newspaper with a grand name as in reality it only reported on around a third of the counties news with other publications serving residents in east and west Lancashire. Headquartered almost directly opposite the bank and adjacent to Marks and Spencer a team of reporters supported by camera men had followed events throughout the day with seasoned reporters reluctant to leave the windows even to use the toilet fearing they would miss one of the biggest news stories Preston had seen in recent years.

The headline of the first edition took almost the whole front page of the newspaper calling out "Armed Police Surround Bank in town centre stand off" but by the time the final edition was printed the story had evolved to "Violent Armed Gang evade Police with £1.2m" and a mystery that was to remain unsolved for 10 years was the topic of dinner table, pub and workplace conversations for weeks and months to come.

Chapter 8   June 1997 Giza Egypt

Mariam stared down from the window of her hotel room at the "Holiday Giza Inn" almost opposite the front gates to the sphinx where bus loads of tourist were dropped off each day seeking another "tick" on their to do list whilst in Egypt. Whilst not an Egyptologist, Mariam was a competent tour guide able to bring stories to life for the visitors to her country, but as she looked out on this searing hot day she still struggled to understand why anyone would visit the main sites in the heat of an Egyptian summers day. When she was working in and around Cairo she always stayed at this hotel as its location was perfect and although it was desperately in need of refurbishment it was clean and had everything she needed for her stays, her days could be long with multiple tours in the day and evening and she could be in the room for as little as 6-7 hours.

The streets outside were noisy, it was like an assault on all your senses at the same time with horns, diesel engines revving, the sound of Hawkers selling their wares and on top of this was the mixed smell of restaurant food cooking and rotting rubbish piled up in the back alleys. Most of the tourists were Americans and Europeans who to her frustration remained fixated on the cheap trinkets in the stores rather than listening to Egyptian history and understanding the dynasties that had once ruled this land. It still amazed her that many tourists arrived thinking there were only 3 pyramids in Egypt and she wished she could have had a dollar for every time she saw a shocked face when she explained there were 9 pyramids at Giza alone and 180 across Egypt and even more beyond the borders and in to the Sudan. As she looked out she found it ironic that she could see such disorganisation in the streets, chaotic scenes in this country once so advanced and civilised, each car fought for space on the road at the same time dodging pedestrians and the horse drawn Kalesch's who pursued the tourist trade.

What was also often a surprise to tourists was that the pyramids at Giza were bordered on one side by the city so if you took your photos on one side you got a desert backdrop but from the other side of the pyramids the view was across to the edge of the city where she stood now.

Mariam was brought up in a devout Muslim family but by her own admission considered herself lapsed although she still followed the faith when she could, on leaving school she had attended Cairo University for three years qualifying in business studies and tourism but then struggled to find employment. At 21 she had started working for the Al Kahil family in Sadat City, Al Kahil himself had started his business on these very streets eventually opening a clothing store then going on to become a media and retail mogul known throughout the world. At first she had started in a role well below her qualified status but her hard work and enterprise had been recognised with her eventually becoming a close aide to Al Kahil and his family. By the early 1990's she was one of the families most trusted employees and spent much of her time shuttling backwards and forwards between Egypt and the south of France where the family had a number of villas and tended to moor their yacht. Although on different continents and culturally worlds apart it was a regular short hop across the Mediterranean that she had grown to know well.

But being around a family of entrepreneurs had made her consider her own hopes and dreams and she had left their employ some two years ago to set up her own travel business but the business had not grown as hoped due to a number of attacks on tourists in Luxor and Aswan that had badly affected the tourist trade to Egypt. But the Government had invested heavily in additional security and as could be seen in the street in front of the hotel the tourists were starting to return in numbers.

It was 5pm and the majority of tourists had headed back to their 5 star hotels and there would be a brief lull on the streets before tourists started to return for the evening sound and light show held in various languages in front of the Sphinx each evening, as much as it was a tourist trap Mariam never tired of seeing the Sphynx and pyramids lit up to the sound of classical music. Mariam turned back in to her room and sat by the small wooden dressing table where she applied a little make up, despite spending almost all her life in sunny climates she would quite easily pass for a European with her fair skin and light mousey blonde hair in contrast to many of her fellow Egyptian women who tended to have black hair and olive skin. Only today she had heard a couple in her tour group debating whether she had British or German origins and although she didn't comment she spoke inwardly to herself that she was proud to be 100% Egyptian. Tonight she was heading to a floating restaurant called Nile City moored on the Nile itself close to Tahrir square but on the opposite bank. She dressed modestly in a long dress and headscarf and low heels carrying a shawl and handbag and blended in with the other locals as she left the hotel and took a bus in to Cairo city centre.

The call from her former colleague at the Al Kahil family had come out of the blue, she had returned from a busy day with a tour group to find the message with a number left at reception for her, at first she hadn't called as she wanted time to consider the reason for the contact but curiosity had gotten the better of her and two days later she had contacted her former male colleague who when she was employed had been a regular security presence with the family but had now been put in the position of heading up the whole of Al Kahils security detail. This was a big responsibility for a young man with occasional rumours that Kahil himself was involved with Mossad and other security services on both sides of the Atlantic as well as being a prominent figure amongst leaders in the Middle East and North Africa.

She had suggested meeting close to the main entrance of the American University in Cairo which itself fronted on to Tahrir square, something told her they should be discrete and it certainly was frowned on for a young woman to meet a man alone in a restaurant and she didn't want to attract that sort of attention. The University would be busy in the early evening with young men and women coming and going and they would attract little attention there. From the University it would only be a 15 minute walk across the Nile and along the embankment to the restaurant which attracted a mixture of local and tourist trade alike.

She had decided to stand by the statue of independence on the other side of the road from the University so she could see him approach then cross to meet him when she saw it was him. It just felt better than waiting in full view outside the University gates and as much as she was looking forward to renewing acquaintances she still had some doubts about the meeting, something she could not put her finger on was nagging away at the back of her brain. She saw him approaching from the Al Tahrir street direction with a purposeful walk, she guessed he had travelled on the cities efficient but overcrowded metro system which continued to develop across the city. She had joked with him once that his looks were more Arabic than her own, he tanned easily and had spent part of his military service in warm climates and if he had grown a moustache to complement his dark hair and dark skin no-one in Cairo would ever have guessed he was British, his purposeful walk and the way he held himself did point to his military background however and she smiled to herself as he reached their meeting point and she carefully negotiated the busy traffic to cross the road to meet him.

They greeted in the traditional local way before turning and heading back down Al Tahrir Street and across Qasr Al Nil Bridge to the west side of the city, as they crossed the bridge she looked back at the Ritz Carlton Hotel and Egyptian Museum admiring their architecture and contrasting bright colours lit up against the dark sky and polluted streets. On the other side of the Nile they soon found the restaurant sitting away from tourists on an upper deck in the corner, she laughed to herself as to why she was being so careful but from the minute she had set eyes on him walking towards the University she knew she was glad she had returned the call and agreed to meet her former colleague and British friend Chris.

At the end of the evening they had crossed back over the Nile on the 6th October Bridge and she had walked to the Bus Park to find transport back to Giza whilst

Chris headed to the Ramses hotel on the Corniche where he said he needed to collect a colleague. It had been a very interesting evening with Chris confirming things about the Al Kahil family she had already thought to be true, after a brief period swapping polite conversation and news Chris had soon turned to business and suggested an offer to her that might be very hard to turn down. As she watched him head through the main entrance and in to the Ramses hotel she realised she had a giddy feeling that was making her heart beat faster and legs skip along like an excited child, it was a heady mix of excitement and danger and as Chris disappeared she realised she had no idea why she thought it might be dangerous and what that danger might be. Despite their different backgrounds and childhoods on different continents, they had always found a lot in common. Chris was quiet and respectful but full of dry humour often teasing her about her beliefs in a non- threatening way, and he had the ability to always make her smile once she began to understand him. He used to jokingly call her El Amira using the European translation for her in deference to her looks and Amira being the Arabic translation of Princess. In return she used to call him Al Wahid Hadi or the quiet one realising they only used these pet names when they were alone referring to each other by their normal names when in the company of other employees. She thought there was something between them but respected the fact that neither had ever crossed that line, a small part of her rather hoped Al

Wahid Hadi or Chris had contacted her purely for reasons of friendship but she knew from the start this would be unlikely.

As the bus weaved its way back to Giza she reflected on the evening and knew that if she took up the offer from Chris on behalf of the Kahil family that life may never be the same again.

Chapter 9   June 1997 London

Peter walked along the Thames from Greenwich to Westminster Bridge where he met friends each Sunday, during the summer months he tended to walk there and get a bus or train back to his home in New Cross. From Greenwich walking along the South Bank of the Thames it was clear to see how London was rapidly changing, old wharves were giving way to trendy apartments and flats with the old and the new sitting sometimes uncomfortably side by side. To the East of Greenwich he could just make out the construction site that had sprung up in an area due to be turned in to sustainable residential and leisure facilities with the centre piece rumoured to be a huge dome to celebrate the forthcoming new millennium. As he walked to the West along the riverside walk he passed old and new London, on the north bank Canary Wharf and the Docklands area continued to develop with historical places of interest mixed in with new metal clad and glazed buildings. The South Bank still hadn't caught up and there was a mixture of small boatyards and abandoned pubs and warehouses where once dockers had welcomed ships and cargo from all over the world. In places the riverside walk came inland and through some of the estates of Rotherhithe and Bermondsey before meeting the river again as it wound its way up towards the Pool of London and Tower Bridge.

His favourite part of the walk was from the tobacco warehouses just east of Tower Bridge then Tower Bridge itself where on very rare occasions he saw the bascules open to let through a small cruise liner or other merchant vessel that would dock against HMS Belfast. Next to Tower Bridge was St Katherines Dock where if time allowed Pete liked to sit and have a pint and imagine what the view would have been like 100 years before. Continuing back on the south bank the path became much busier passing many tourist attractions and the ongoing construction work to develop the Tate Gallery and the Globe where several hundred years before Shakespeare's plays had been performed. Looking across to the north bank iconic buildings such as St Pauls Cathedral and the Tower of London could be seen and Pete literally felt that history was reaching out to him.

As he approached the old County Hall building once home to the Greater London Council he marvelled at the architecture and studied the land where it was said a huge Ferris wheel was to be built also to coincide with the forthcoming millennium celebrations. On the other bank was the jewel in the crown, the Palace of Westminster containing the House of Lords, Commons and ancillary supporting buildings. For hundreds of years decisions had been made here that affected everyone not just here in Britain but also across the world, at one point one third of the world's population was governed from here and many countries around the world had chosen the "Westminster System" as their choice of governance.

At this point he left the path and headed down Westminster Bridge Road passing under the railway arches that took the main railway out of Waterloo station, one of the busiest commuter stations anywhere in the world. Here the architecture changed, a little more run down as the road headed towards the Elephant and Castle and eventually the Old Kent Road which in its day was the main route out to the south coast and Europe. Before this though he turned off in to Hercules Road and walked towards the Pineapple pub, despite its name this was a proper South London local that served office workers on weekday lunches but in the evening came alive with locals relaxing after a busy day's work, although the landscape was changing this was true cockney territory with the Lambeth Walk only a few hundred yards away. Just round the corner was the MI6 building which for a few years Pete had viewed as just another office building only to find out it was home to the UK's battle against international espionage, this had been one of his many discoveries as he worked for the shadow government on matters of security.

Tonight there were five of them meeting up which meant that quite a few drinks would flow, the Pineapple had two bars, a traditional saloon where locals would chat, play pool and darts and a more comfortable lounge where locals mixed with visitors with music playing in the background. As he approached Pete reflected on the way his friendships had developed and the friends he met tonight were different from Colin, Chris, Dave and John in that they came from different areas of the country with different beliefs and ambitions, he missed that he didn't see his old comrades quite as often but also felt more at home with his new circle of friends. Tonight he would go easy on the beer as in the morning he had an early flight to Aberdeen then onwards to Sumburgh on the Shetland islands, from there Dave's Dad would collect him and take him to Bressay where he was due to spend a week.

Since the late 1980's Pete felt he had been able to be more open about his sexuality and had opened up to select friends about his feelings, however he had not been brave enough to broach the subject with his conservative family and on the rare visits home his Mum still talked of suitable girlfriends for him and he knew one day soon he would need to have those awkward conversations with family and certain friends.

Every time he plucked up courage something somewhere would be said that shattered his confidence. Several weeks ago Colin had visited for a long weekend as their local football team were playing in London, initial enthusiasm for the weekend had dampened somewhat when Colin had become drunk on the first night and abused two guys who he had seen holding hands on the street, not only this he had continued to use homophobic language all the way back to Pete's flat. Despite this Pete did value the friendship and felt it was just twentysomething bravado and with some education Colin may change his views, indeed he wondered whether the outward homophobia masked feelings that Colin didn't want to share with anyone, after all Pete could not remember Colin ever mentioning a girlfriend.

Colin had really embraced the Manchester music scene which had spawned bands such as the Stone roses, Inspiral Carpets and Happy Mondays and then eventually Oasis. He had done really well for himself and was a bit of a mystery on the business scene in Preston where he already operated two pub/clubs with live music appearing most weeks at the age of 26. Colin himself had been talented musically and enjoyed giving local bands a stage to promote themselves and his Sunday night open mic sessions had become legendary in Preston. He had cut the weekend short to return home on the Sunday afternoon as a band with lots of potential were due to perform and he was determined not to miss them. Pete had travelled up to London Euston station with Colin on the Sunday and they had enjoyed lunch together before he had joined an afternoon train back to Preston, Pete had been amazed to see him walk up to the ticket office and simply buy a first class ticket home without batting an eyelid, yes Colin really seemed to have made it financially.

Back in the Pineapple Pub the conversation was focussed on politics and elections that constitutionally would have to take place in the next 12 months, Pete was hopeful that this would be his big chance and with the traditionally left leaning labour party moving towards the centre of British politics the conclusion was that the forthcoming election results were just a formality. This was another awkward conversation he needed to have with his family who were all traditionally conservative voters with views over to the right of the house and had been involved in politics at a local level for many years. He wasn't sure which announcement would cause them most angst, their son being gay or their son crossing to the rival party. The switch had been easy for Pete as his own views developed in the late 1980's and brutal infighting amongst the conservatives had led to him making the switch early in 1992.

Whilst the party had embraced Pete and his computer like brain he still hadn't told anyone other than close colleagues the truth about his sexuality, he had had a near miss only a year after joining the party when he had been in the Royal Vauxhall Tavern in South London watching an up and coming drag artist. The tavern was a well known gay venue with a busy live music and performing scene, for years they had been victims of Police prejudice and he had been there when an up and coming drag artist was performing and the venue had been raided by Police wearing rubber gloves. A number of regular customers had been arrested and although no charges were forthcoming Pete knew their names, which would now be held somewhere on a database, something he was desperate to avoid himself. It had been a narrow escape and so unfair for everyone given that the regulars were harming no-one and simply enjoying their evenings, victimised because of their sexuality. The press had arrived once they heard about the raid but Pete was confident that he had escaped before the cameras started snapping which was relief as the raid was front page headline news on the following day's Evening Standard newspaper, which although London focussed had a readership some national media would be envious of.

He spent a pleasant night in the Pineapple with his friends before heading off early as he had promised himself, a short walk to the takeaway then a 53 bus took him almost all the way to his door step. The 5am morning alarm call shocked him back in to life and after dressing he took a taxi to London City airport which had handily been built on old converted docks just a short drive from his home. Not only was it convenient geographically it also didn't have the queues and bustle of London's larger airports and Pete liked to think of it as London's secret transport gem. For the third time he checked the file he had with him. Over the years Pete had continued to visit Dave once a year and only two years ago he had realised that Dave had become a complete computer expert. Whether it was repairing machines, developing programmes or breaking codes very little was beyond Dave and with his limited mobility he spent much of his day working on his PC. Pete had managed to engage Dave on a contract with the party based on a rate for each assignment meaning he could guarantee the work was done efficiently, competently and with the utmost discretion. Based on the last assignment Pete had suggested Dave relocating to London and being closer to the decision makers of Whitehall but Dave had refused, instead quoting his quality of life as the major reason for not wanting to move away from his family and the friends he had made. In fact Dave was insistent that in the future most people would work from home with the development in technology rendering the office a relic of the past, his ideas were often shot down in business with organisations majoring on Dave's own mobility issues saying they biased his thinking. But Pete thought Dave had something with his views, in the years he had known him and particularly the last few years as he matured Dave had never been wrong with any of his predictions, indeed if his own political ambitions developed as he hoped, he wanted Dave to be his confidante, the government needed people who worked and thought differently, and worked in ways that others didn't yet understand.

As he walked out of the tiny terminal at Sumburgh he saw Dave's Dad waiting and raise his hand in a genuinely warm greeting, the tiny airport was mainly used by oil workers arriving to work off shore or returning after weeks on a rig, as remote as the Shetlands were, strangers attracted little attention here as there was such a transient workforce – perfect for what Pete had planned. Plane to car took less than ten minutes with no formalities to complete and because you literally grabbed your luggage from the side of the plane and obviously no immigration after the internal flight. A 30 minute drive saw them in Lerwick where after picking up some groceries from the CO-OP store they took the short crossing on the ferry from Lerwick to Bressay where they dropped off supplies for the Maryfield House Hotel which offered rooms as well as a small public bar and then continued to the small crofters farm where he saw Dave sat outside waiting.

Over a pot of tea Dave and Pete caught up on their news and like the old friends they were they immediately both felt like they had last spoken only the day before. They headed out on one of the few roads on the island with Dave independently refusing to be pushed by Pete, it was a windy day as they talked urgently with Dave keen to know what Pete had done with the data he had recovered from his last visit but he was being somewhat elusive instead focussing on the latest data he had brought on the journey. They both looked out across a grey and murky northernmost area of the north sea watching a bulk fuel carrier head out from the islands, there was no-one in earshot and if there had been any noise would have been extinguished by the swirling wind but Dave still felt the need to whisper when he spoke to Pete. Dave realised what he had discovered amongst the data was explosive and potentially could change the British establishment for ever if things developed, but as he explained this to Pete he also knew his friend was right to say this was dangerous information to own and that for now they both needed to continue to trust each other. As the sky's darkened Pete reached down and embraced Dave, he had trusted him with his biggest personal secret and he knew he could trust him with this as well. Secrets involving the Royal Family and Politicians were always explosive, but this was pure dynamite.

Chapter 10   June 1997 North Yorkshire

Royal Air Force Menwith Hill is an RAF station near Harrogate in North Yorkshire which in reality is almost 100% operated by US intelligence agencies which it has done since it's purchase back in 1954. In the 1980's it had created news as protestors had camped outside believing there to be nuclear connections but the reality is the main focus is missile warning and communication intercepts. Whilst the UK government retains ownership and a small element of control, the truth is the base is one cog of a connection of three bases around the world with the other two being in the US and Australia. Listening Antennae are housed in around 40 extensive "randomes" which locals who pass the base regularly refer to as "the golf balls", rumour has it that despite few people outside the area being aware of its existence, RAF Menwith Hill is the biggest facility of its kind in the world.

The base is set out like an American town with its own Main Street containing diners, a cinema, bowling alley and school with estimates of 1500 staff being on base at any one time. Being only 6 miles west of Harrogate, Americans not living on base chose to live in Harrogate itself or the surrounding villages meaning it was not uncommon to hear American accents or see left hand drive cars in this quintessential English town. Menwith Hill was believed to be part of the joint

UK/US/Australian echelon eavesdropping system although each government offered a polite no comment when requests for information were made.

Pete had left the Shetlands after a short stay and his boss had arranged a visit to the base at Menwith Hill as part of the parties preparation for Government. After the short flight to Aberdeen and a bus in to the city he had taken the train down the East Coast passing St Andrews and some of the most spectacular links golf courses anywhere in the world over the Forth Bridge and in to Edinburgh. After a short break he had taken the train south to York and just over two hours later was being met by his American host outside York railway station from where they would make the 45 minute journey to Menwith Hill. This was all part of the labour parties plan to reach out to close allies in advance of the forthcoming elections, the prime-minister was determined to appear as a party switched on to world affairs with the ability to govern a global player which they had not always demonstrated in the past. Politically they were very close in their beliefs to the Clinton administration in the US and as main researcher for the shadow defence minister this trip was set to be one of his most important in the lead in to hopefully taking power the following year.

His host/driver certainly wasn't giving much away and Pete guessed that communication in the car may be monitored anyway so after 15 minutes he sat back and chuckled to himself that he was receiving a guided tour of the local area from an American despite himself being born in the adjacent county Lancashire. After skirting Harrogate it was an easy 10 minute drive down the A59 main road to Menwith Hill where they entered a security holding area so the car and its contents could be scanned before they were allowed in to the outer base area.

Pete's first impressions were like many in the area, this was very much an American operation, the car park was even full of left hand drive cars and they had an American style "Fire Department". Although there were known to be a team from the UK governments communication specialist at GCHQ you literally would have thought you had landed on American soil. His host was a tall man who introduced himself as Dale from Leavenworth, Kansas, it always fascinated Pete why Americans introduced themselves with both their town/city and state whereas in the UK most people would just say their town/city. As they headed off round the base in a Jeep SUV Dale made small talk about baseball and the Kansas City Royals chances of success this year and explained how he had attended his first "English" cricket match but hadn't come to terms with the pace or the rules. In return Pete asked about Leavenworth and in particular the military prison also making small talk about crop returns in Kansas, after all it was often described as the bread basket of America. Pete didn't learn too much from the visit other than the scale of the facility and the obvious pride all the us Ex-pats had in their home from home right here on the Yorkshire Moors. The route they took was obviously well rehearsed and as he was driven off-base he was just left thinking that the partnership was only a partnership when either country wanted it to be.

As he was dropped off at Harrogate from where he planned to take the train to Leeds then onwards to Preston, one thing was left spinning round his head. As he pulled in to the drop off area at Harrogate station he was certain the driver had said "what was Pete's view on there being a Muslim prince in the royal lineage in the future", what an odd thing to say he thought.

Although only a journey of 70 miles it was almost 3 hours later when the train rattled in to Preston as the trans Pennine route took in the Yorkshire mill towns before passing through spectacular scenery on the border with Lancashire then dropping down through the mill towns of East Lancashire then finally joining the main line on the approach to Preston. He was instantly reminded of that fateful day in October 1984 when the train had failed to stop at a red light and Dave's life had changed forever. He also reflected that Preston station had changed very little from that fateful day too, well over a decade on there were less routes operating and those that did generally took longer, progress indeed! He hoped that as a rising young star of the political party about to gain power that he would be able to play some part in evening out transport investment across the UK.

He had 15 minutes to kill before the local train to Leyland so walked across to the newsagents to pick up the Lancashire Evening Post, it was more out of habit really as the local stories of any regional paper bore little relevance to his life in Westminster. The back pages were previewing another football season and his local team were being predicted to gain promotion from the bottom league as fortunes looked like they would turn at last. By the time he reached Leyland he had pretty much finished with the newspaper so before leaving the train he put on his Walkman and then after disembarking made the short journey home to his parents. After a scolding for being later than he had promised he had a cup of tea before settling down in his bedroom that was pretty much as he had left it when he moved down to London, he knew his parents would keep it in this condition until he finally owned his own bricks and mortar. Whilst he was tempted to read he knew also he had a busy day the next day and would no doubt get a grilling from his Mum in the morning so instead he turned off the light and closed his eyes, but sleep wouldn't come and over and over again in his mind he heard an American Mid-West drawl "what was Pete's view on there being a Muslim prince in the royal lineage in the future", "what was Pete's view on there being a Muslim prince in the royal lineage in the future", "what was Pete's view on there being a Muslim prince in the royal lineage in the future".

The next morning was a perfect summers day and from his parents back window he could see the flat arable fields on the moss looking west, Leyland was growing and his Mum was bending his ear about this view disappearing for good if the local labour council let another new housing development go ahead, although he hadn't told them too much about his role his Mum and Dad definitely thought he had friends in high places, he would have to let them down gently.

He had arranged to meet up with John today, he was working out of Heysham still but had transferred on to the King Orry, the Isle of Man ferry as his career had developed and was currently working on an apprenticeship with the ferry company that with the right application and mentoring could lead to him becoming a Master and ultimately in overall control of the flagship ferry on the historic routes between the Isle of Man and the mainland ports. The ferry really was a lifeline with two crossings a day carrying the fresh produce, freight, tourists and islanders travelling between the mainland and their home. The crossing took around 3 ½ hours and continued every day in all but the harshest of conditions. Although on the face of it working on the ferry looked somewhat repetitive the changing weather and the difficult navigation around the ports at either end meant you could never rest if you were on watch. As well as the staple crossings to the mainland there were seasonal links from the island to both the North and South of Ireland and the coastal resorts of North Wales. The Isle of Man and its residents (known as Manx) were fiercely independent, in various laws of the United Kingdom, the UK is defined to exclude the Isle of Man. Historically, the UK has taken care of its external and defence affairs, and retained paramount power to legislate for the Island. However, it had been mooted that the Isle of Man and the UK would in future sign an agreement that established frameworks for the development of the international identity of the Isle of Man. However there was currently no separate Manx citizenship which is covered by UK law, and Manx people are classed as British citizens. There is a long history of relations and cultural exchange between the Isle of Man and Ireland and the Isle of Man's historic Manx language are closely related to both Scottish Gaelic and the Irish language. Many people on the mainland couldn't even pinpoint the island on a map despite its size and those that did know it generally linked it with its advantageous tax laws that saw many individuals and businesses take up residence on the island to avoid the harsher UK tax laws.

Although John was off shift today he started early the following day so had declined the offer of a few drinks in either Lancaster or Preston and instead suggested they walked around the Glasson Dock area. Pete had never learned to drive like his friends as in London he had always felt a car was a liability with the amount of traffic and the lack of places to park either at home or his workplace. So instead Pete caught the train up to Lancaster and John drove in from Glasson Dock where he still lived and they walked together along the Lune. Whilst remaining friends throughout, Pete and John had probably been the least close amongst the group but equally where little cracks had appeared in friendships amongst the group of school friends this had meant they had never fallen out either.

As they walked into a strong Westerly breeze they talked openly about their careers, dreams and any blockers that were stopping them getting to where they wanted to be. As conversation turned to their other friends they both commented that they had not heard from Chris for over a year and neither had they heard of him being home in the North West and they both promised each other to pass on news if they heard anything. Pete was genuinely interested in John's career and how he lived his life and had hundreds of questions about the Isle of Man which he had never visited himself, but John had chuckled saying that although he visited the island sometimes ten times a week he rarely disembarked at the other side unless there was a specific operational reason or a training course he had to attend.

John and Pete had kept themselves in shape despite their job roles not involving manual work, they had walked along the old railway line towards Glasson at a pace most people would consider as jogging and were now stood on the headland where the River Lune met the Irish Sea. The early afternoon ferry to the Isle of Man was just leaving Heysham out into Morecambe Bay and Pete was interested to hear about the logistics of the difficult navigation this entailed from John as well as his obvious pride for what he had achieved and the people he sailed with. The King Orry was an ageing ferry but perfect for the route due to its smaller size and side loading ability meaning it could dock pretty much anywhere in the island or west cost of the UK if needed, whilst a new ferry was currently being built the King Orry would continue on the route for some years to come.

John explained that one of his roles was to assess the weight of each loading before the crossing and sometimes this entailed making priority decisions and leaving cargo behind in the summer months rather than put the crossing at risk whereas in the winter with lower passenger numbers there was more room for freight.

Currently, John had explained, a middle eastern family had bought an old military airfield on the island known as Jurby and intended to redevelop the area as well as moving their European head office for their operations to the island. Each day a 40 foot container would arrive at Heysham by trailer and its own tractor unit returning the following day empty as some members of the family and employees started to set up their base on the island. The story fascinated Pete as tax avoidance was becoming a big issue and one the current government was struggling to clamp down on, without appearing too inquisitive Pete asked about the company and family that were relocating to the Isle of Man, John said he couldn't remember the family name but he thought the owner had just purchased a football team in London, so possibly from the middle east.

Pete decided to jog the 8 miles back to Lancaster rather than wait for the irregular bus service, it gave him some serious thinking time which he felt he needed. He had taken the role in the party as a rising star but through a series of coincidences and piecing together a number of pieces of a jigsaw he never asked for, he felt he was in the middle of a story that could rock the establishment more violently than the abdication of the Queens Uncle some 60 years ago. As he neared Lancaster he took out his mobile phone pulled up the aerial and dialled his boss, mobile coverage was still very patchy in the North West but he needed to talk to someone

Chapter 11   August 1997 Port Grimaud France

Chris walked amongst the low and mid rise buildings of Port Grimaud on one of the hottest days of the year with temperatures over 35 Celsius. "The boss" was due in town early in the evening with his jet flying into Nice and then a short hop by helicopter to the villa built on reclaimed swamps just outside the town. He would probably spend the night at the Villa before transferring to his private yacht the Dianawa which he planned to spend the week on hugging the coast of the Mediterranean arriving in Monaco for the Formula 1 Grand Prix the following Saturday.

Despite its outward appearance it was only around thirty years since planning permission had been given to build Port Grimaud, a dream of the visionary architect from the Alsace region Francois Spoerry, who had helped to create this modern-day, lakeside city. A fan of gentle architecture, that is to say he was opposed to the large, regular-shaped, rectilinear structures that were popular at that time. And so Port-Grimaud had been born with its surreal sense of space and mid-rise buildings so popular in Provence and in keeping with the existing, surrounding buildings.

Tourists on package holidays tended to head to St Tropez to see the millionaires yachts and promenade round the harbour but the reality was that most of the super rich avoided St Tropez like the plague for that very reason preferring places like Port Grimaud or simply anchoring out at sea sending staff in for supplies when needed.

Chris reached the Dianawa which was currently being prepared by the Al Kahil sailing staff ready for its forthcoming voyage. Built only 10 years before especially for the family it could house up to 16 people across 8 staterooms in addition to rooms for its 20 crew members. Dianawa contained a jacuzzi, swim platform, sun deck, a formal dining room, main saloon, a bar, and office space so the family could relax yet stay connected to their various business ventures. Despite only being built recently it was full of dark wood panelling and coffered ceilings with the interior reminiscent of the Arts and Crafts style of the early 1900s. The yacht was powered by four Wartsila engines, and had a cruising speed of 15 knots and top speed of 20 knots costing $15m when built, Chris had recently overseen a £0.5m security upgrade giving the family additional privacy and an advanced warning system that analysed approaching craft.

Tonight though Chris was more interested in the adjacent craft looking for anything unusual and considering who would be overlooking "the boss" and his guests when he embarked tomorrow. Given the layout of Port Grimaud the approach to the yacht was very hard to secure and it wasn't possible to get a vehicle close to the yacht as it had to be moored in the outer harbour given its size. But there didn't appear to be anything out of the ordinary and the yachts that were occupied tended to contain just a few occupants, most of them lounging around or enjoying drinks on deck. But Chris knew that someone willing to commit harm would be unlikely to be sat there advertising it, with the global political stretch of his empire and vast wealth the boss was a definite target and anyone wanting to harm him would be likely to hire the best to do the job. When Al Kahil had called he had said there would be the normal family members boarding plus one special guest codenamed KP, the guest would need extra vigilance on their behalf but covertly not overtly, this was someone who attracted the media of the world and for Chris, still relatively young in his career, it took things to a totally different level.

Despite dreaming about a long military career things hadn't gone the way Chris had planned, he had left the army at the first opportunity following the Derry incident on Inniscarn Road back in December 1988. Initially he had been labelled a hero by his regiment after dashing in to the burning house and single handed protecting the residents whilst also putting down covering fire so his fellow soldiers could reach cover and shortly after all were extricated without any significant injury by an evacuation patrol. He had returned to barracks immediately after the event and spent December 1988 in Preston, that month had been spent with family and friends and a series of interviews with regiment colleagues about his conduct on that day. Whilst it was widely accepted his conduct had saved his colleagues from injury or worse, it was regularly put to him that he had gone against his commanding officer's orders. Whilst the outcome of the investigations resulted in no action he felt his card had been marked and career progression was going to be difficult so in 1991 be found himself back on civvy street and after two months out of work he had accepted a role in a private security firm run by ex-military sorts then eventually working for Al Kahil where his career had advanced rapidly under the watchful eyes of an ex US Navy seal Jay Romme. When Romme had retired Chris was offered the role heading up Al Kahils security and whilst many at his age may have balked at the challenge Chris had instead lapped up every opportunity and been ruthless in surrounding himself with the best in the business rather than people who simply thought and acted like he did.

He had become distant from his family who were disappointed in his decision to leave the military but with him now resident outside the UK he thought little about it. He found himself mainly in the south of France, Paris and North Africa with the ability to travel on multiple passports provided by his boss, he had his own villa, the pick of the bosses' cars and a lifestyle and salary he could only ever have dreamed of. Of his friends from school he remained relatively close to Pete and Colin but even that amounted to no more than a few phone calls a year and the chance of a quick pint on his rare visits to the UK, he was supremely fit and worked out both at the bosses gym in Port Grimaud but almost daily with runs on the beach or off in to the olive tree clad hills that rose in to Provence from Port Grimaud.

Ironically the time at home in late 1988 hadn't done anything to improve the relationship with Jackie who was set on following the various rites of passage of UK University life. They had split amicably and he had had no contact since, Chris wasn't a sentimental person and saw little value in keeping up pretences.

When he first started work with Kahil he had met Mariam who had worked with the family for several years, they had bonded and Chris had felt this was a relationship that may flourish. Although not the strictest follower of her faith the family, he felt, had not been supportive of their fledgling relationship and when she had left Al Kahils employment to pursue opportunities at home he had been disappointed but not sad.

He had not often thought of Mariam and it had been a complete surprise when Kahil had suggested approaching her to bring her back in to "the business", the boss felt that that the new connections in the family, and in particular his sons new girlfriend, put additional pressure on the staff and Mariam had managed things very efficiently in the past with her impassive nature and ability to blend in to European and North African cultures. He had spotted her in Cairo when he recce'd the area just before they met, as glad as he had been to see her clearly alone and looking alert there had been nothing emotional on his side but he had very much looked forward to sparring with her again in the brother/sister way they had in the past, he smiled to himself as he thought about how much fun it would be to have El Amira back in the fold and working closely with him.

Romantically though Chris had met someone three years before whilst on a trip with Al Kahil to Nairobi, Aimee had been their liaison at Nairobi University where the boss was looking to invest and despite all his security responsibilities he hadn't been able to resist some flirtatious communications after the visit. He had found Aimee to be somewhat mysterious with her dual passports and roots both in the Sudan and Uganda whilst working in Kenya. He realised from the feelings she brought from within him that he had never really loved before, she was cute beyond belief with the sexiest of smiles and shyest of expressions and she had totally stolen his heart. Like him she had a very active mind and they had found common interests in geo-political situations and had spent one whole evening and in to the small hours making a bucket list of countries they both wanted to visit.

Unfortunately despite their shared love of world geography it also created challenges for them both with them living and working on separate continents but Aimee had often joked with him that when they did meet up the feelings it brought in her were of volcanic proportions. As he walked round the jetty's of Port Grimaud he allowed himself a small smile as he thought of her last visit and how they had run together on the beach before she had returned to the airport at Nice and onwards back to Africa. He remembered her huge smile and wave as she had disappeared through departures and he was reminded of her lying on his chest as she did often through the night snoring lightly before disappearing off in to the bed when he dreams became deeper and more vivid. She was due to visit again soon and he knew he wanted to convince her to move to Europe but he just didn't know how the conversation should start, but what he did know was that he wanted to spend the rest of his life with this beautiful positive bundle of energy as close to him as possible.

Chris finished his tour of the jetty's and the yachts tied up moving gently in the light evening breeze, he scanned the properties and rooftops of the adjacent quayside and decided that as far as he could see there were no dangers at this stage. His phone buzzed and he removed it from his pocket and took the call, it was on the private network available only to the family so he knew it would be one of his security detail calling to say they were not far from Port Grimaud, indeed it turned out they were closer than he thought and the inauspicious looking Landover Discovery could soon be seen winding down towards the port and within minutes Al Kahil his wife, son and security detail were exiting the vehicle. He was frustrated to see that Karim the security team member assigned to the trip had been sat in the additional seats in the trunk of the vehicle, this would have given him poor visibility and no ability to exit the vehicle quickly in an emergency situation, small details were important and this wasn't even a small detail, Chris didn't like being undermined but Al Kahil had been insistent that they would take one vehicle and he would drive himself, Chris mused that at least it did look like a low profile arrival as he had recommended.

Al Kahil's son Dada had exited the vehicle and quickly ran to the other side where he opened the door for his relatively new girlfriend, they walked with purpose round the vehicle and towards Chris, he had often found Dada difficult and almost a complete opposite to his father with little humility and frankly often behaving like a spoilt child, but recently he had warmed to him a little and ultimately he had to remain professional as he was an influential member of the family groomed to succeed his father.

As Dada and his girlfriend approached him he saw her for the first time, even with her modest clothing, sunglasses and peaked cap she stood out, there was somehow a stature and poise he hadn't seen before, she was one of the most photographed people in the world and as she stepped on to gangplank to board the Dianawa he realised that like many before him he himself was completely overawed to be so close to her. Dada had aimed high and had hit the jackpot, whilst the family were no shrinking violets, bringing Lady Diana The Princess of Wales in to the family was going to take things to a totally different level.

Chapter 12   August 1997 Preston

Colin stood on the pitch at Deepdale as his beloved football team Preston North End went through their preseason photo shoot, he looked round the stadium and marvelled at how he had once stood on the terraces and dreamed of playing for the club but was now stood here as a shareholder rubbing shoulders with directors, players and other officials. The club had been on its knees for a few years with attendances falling, the stadium needing investment and some pretty poor performances on the pitch. All this had led to the team finding themselves in the bottom league of the professional game in England for the second time in a decade with debts piling up. Colin was one of a few local businessmen who had committed not just money but business acumen too and the previous season had seen the team promoted as champions in to the level above but also importantly investment in the stadium which was now being redeveloped to be at the heart of the towns regeneration. His involvement had led to more questions than he would have liked about his background and where he made his money at such a young age but he had managed to handle these in that way he had of giving lots of information but never answering the question.

On the face of it he was a local success story owning and managing significant leisure facilities across the town and beyond including pubs, a bowling alley and cinema whilst also being in talks with other businessmen to operate the town's theatre complex which like the football stadium had also seen better days. The previous night he had been interviewed by the local regional newspaper which had been digging into his story and he had just read the edited version on the way up to the stadium. They had been reasonably fair and concluded that he would bring benefit both to the rebirth of the football club and leisure facility in town but had left open questions about where he had made his money. Colin didn't care too much he rarely felt the need to conform or explain and certainly wouldn't take much notice of any feedback from readers. His empire was developing quickly and he had certainly benefitted from his father's friend Trev who had mentored him and who himself had a rags to riches story he could share and Colin could learn from.

The week previously Colin had been on the Isle of Man primarily to look at a business opportunity but he had also met a local tax consultant to gain a better understanding of the local laws and in particular the higher tax rate of only 20% which was significantly lower than in the United Kingdom, the mentoring sessions with Trev were already paying dividends. It was his recommendation not to look too far afield when there was a potential tax haven only 70 miles off the coast of his home region. Colin had met the consultant in a pub called "The Prospect" in the business area of

Douglas the "capital" or principal town of the Isle of Man. The prospect was a converted bank opposite the "House of Keys" which was home to the Isle of Man parliament and they had been able to meet and talk inconspicuously with the general buzz of the customers conversation ensuring that discussion about his finances could be kept discrete. It had been particularly ironic Colin had thought to have sat in a pub that had been converted from a large retail bank, he himself had recently purchased the bank where he had once worked and was busy turning it in to a drink, food and dance venue, with the armed robbery of 1988 to reflect on, that building would always be a big part of his life.

Colin had also managed to spend some time with John on the journey over, John was off shift but actually on the King Orry Ferry as it made its morning departure to Heysham. They hadn't caught up for some months so it had been great to learn about how John's career was developing, he had been amazed to see the small bridge where the ship was navigated and controlled from and how such a small team were responsible for this large vessel, its passenger and freight in all weathers. Whilst John was off duty he hadn't deemed it appropriate to sit in the ships bar and drink bearing in mind he was an employee so they had instead sat in the coffee lounge and chewed the fat for a couple of hours. Interestingly also on the crossing had been a number of employees from an international business run by the Egyptian Al Kahil. John had explained that they were relocating some of their business to headquarter it in the UK giving them substantial tax breaks but with the benefit of business with the UK and Ireland right on the doorstep. John even joked that Colin might have competition for investment in his local football club as Al Kahil was known to be looking for a club he could develop to be successful in the newly formed English Premier League. Conversation soon turned to their actual home town of Leyland, whilst Colin had invested heavily in the neighbouring town of Preston their hearts lay in Leyland where they had walked the streets, been involved in all sorts of scrapes and most of all played together as teenagers when they made their pledge to always look out for each other wherever they ended up. Leyland had continued to develop in terms of housing growth although the local infrastructure was not catching up with more transport, schools and medical facilities amongst the things that were lagging behind. The central area where the market had stood for many years was now abandoned and John had heard a rumour that Colin may have purchased some of the land and was interested to know what his plans were. Local media had run a story showing grand plans of a new supermarket, town centre parking all supported by small local shops but they had been unable to get a comment from the new owners of the land, there also seemed to be some mystery about the foreman charged with clearing the abandoned site and in particular the fact he seemed to have disappeared without trace which his family had described as being totally out of character.

John realised for the first time that he actually felt unable to question Colin directly about his plans, there was something in Colin's answers that automatically shut down the question and whilst he had that familiar smile on his face his eyes didn't smile or sparkle at all.

A late breakfast arrived as the ferry entered Morecambe bay around an hour away from its destination, they had both chosen Manx Kippers whose serving were a hundred year old tradition on the ferry. Manx Kippers have a unique flavour from a century old tradition of taking herring fillets which are then hung for 8 hours drawing out the oils as they absorb the seasoning in the traditional smokehouse. They had both tucked in to the simple breakfast smothering their fish with butter before finishing off with a mug of hot tea just before the ferry docked.

Within ten minutes both friends were on the quayside at Heysham and as Colin prepared to leave he shook hands with his old friend John, as John headed back on to the ferry for the return crossing to the island he watched Colin walk off the quay to the small long stay car park and realised that along with the lack of warmth in Colin's smile, the handshake too had been perfunctory and he realised he now had more questions than answers.

As John returned to his staff cabin he decided to catch the local radio news taking advantage of the clear signal whilst they were in port. Grandly calling themselves the voice of the county the midday news on BBC Radio Lancashire led with the story of a discovery of a body in town centre Leyland under the rubble being cleared as part of the market redevelopment, and for some reason a shiver went through John's body and he felt like someone was jumping on his grave.

Chapter 13   August 1997 Port Grimaud France

The Dianawa was gleaming as it headed out of the small port and into the Gulf of St Tropez towards the Mediterranean. Its sleek design but traditional build attracted admiring glances wherever it went and there were many jealous eyes on them from the small pier and other yachts as they slid out into the sea. To all intents and purposes the yacht looked empty as its clever design meant that those on board could relax in the evening sun unseen whilst equally enjoying an unobstructed view of the coastline and out to sea. As well as a small deck pool, seating and loungers there was a covered dining table meaning that dinner could be served al fresco informally without the need to dress for the more formal interior dining room. It was here that Dada entertained his girlfriend safe in the knowledge that their privacy was protected. They passed St Tropez off the starboard side and Sainte Maxime on the port side before heading round the Cap de St Tropez then anchoring in the sheltered Bay de Bonporteau. It wasn't long before Chris got a security warning call from the bridge to head up for a possible breach, whilst they had left Port Grimaud quietly word had soon got round that British Royalty had been spotted boarding a yacht and their position had been tracked with opportune journalists and their camera operators heading to the coastal area nearest to their position out at sea. The yacht had both a covered and uncovered bridge and could also be fully operated form the bridge side wings if necessary, Chris slipped down to the lower uncovered bridge and scanned the shoreline with his binoculars. The team had been right to flag this, whilst not a direct security breach it was clear that with their sophisticated camera equipment they would be able to catch shots of the yachts occupants as they walked around some of the external areas. Whilst security had always been tight given the profile and value of the Kahil family this was a different sort of threat and one for which he needed a new strategy. He returned to the bridge and asked the skipper to arrange a 5am security briefing the following day before loitering on deck to catch Dada on his own away from the princess so as not to cause any alarm. Eventually Dada came along the starboard side and he took the opportunity to brief him on the situation on the shore with the gathered journalists. Dada explained to Chris that they had fully expected some intrusion and he was comfortable with Chris's suggestions and minutes later Chris briefed the skipper to make a seemingly unhurried departure away from the area and out to sea and away from the area to watching eyes for the remainder of the evening, then circle back under the cover of darkness to Port Grimaud where another passenger would be waiting on the quayside at 4am. Given how soon the press had picked up on them being in the area they agreed to anchor in the bay around 3.30am and Chris himself would take the inflatable tender in to Port Grimaud to greet the mystery guest.

The Dianawa gracefully headed approximately south towards the Hyeres isles not far from Toulon and all gathered on deck to see the magnificent August sunset, Chris looked across to the distant shoreline momentarily as he heard the familiar sound of helicopter rotor blades cutting through the air as a machine lifted from Toulouse airport but he relaxed a little when he saw it head inland away from their position. The sound of rotors cutting through the air immediately took him back to his extraction from Northern Ireland after the incident in Londonderry but given the heightened security he needed to lead on he soon snapped himself back in to the moment. He saw the Princess walk on her own to the front of the yacht speaking urgently in to her mobile phone and he pledged to include phone security when he and the crew considered all the security options in the morning.

Eventually the passengers started to retire to their beds and Chris visited the bridge once more to view the course they would take and ascertain whether the skipper had seen any suspicious activity around them on radar. The skipper seemed relaxed and reassured Chris that the only risk he could foresee was chance photographers zooming in on them from the passing roll on roll off car ferry inbound to Toulon from the French island of Corsica. Chris therefore headed down to the crew quarters knowing he could get five hours sleep before he needed to rise and take the tender in to Port Grimaud, the yacht was quiet with the few family passengers taking the opportunity to catch up on sleep following their busy day of travelling. He entered his cabin and after smiling at his bedside picture of Aimee he climbed on to his bed and surprisingly found sleep quickly.

The Dianawa kept up an arching circular route at a speed of 8 knots, the skipper and his coxswain were more than capable of controlling the yacht, monitoring the systems and remaining security aware. It was a clear night and the hot day had given way to a pleasantly cool night which itself would soon give way to dawn, the skipper called down to Chris's cabin to ensure he was ready for the shore transfer but as he put the phone to his ear Chris appeared on the bridge which actually didn't surprise the skipper too much. They were just entering the Gulf of St Tropez and foreward to port the lights of St Tropez could be seen as the late night or early morning revellers continued to party hard then after passing St Tropez Port Grimaud could be seen in the distance, the lighting more subtle but as a result the harbour entrance easier to see with the naked eye. Reducing down to just two knots eventually the skipper dropped the anchor in the bay allowing Chris to head to the stern of the yacht where he pushed off alone in to the early morning light. He had been told the additional passenger would be waiting on quay two, was female and would be expecting him and he may recognise her, Chris had been unclear as to the need for secrecy and inwardly joked with himself that surely they were not collecting another Princess?

Whilst Chris felt not bringing the Dianawa back in to port was the right plan he realised that the outboard motor of the tender was making a significant noise as he approached the harbour so he reduced speed down until he could see quay two and he let the tender drift in the last 250 metres. He had actually risen at 2.30am to make notes about that mornings security briefing and he was already regretting not having a morning coffee to deaden the pain of another night with reduced sleeping hours, Aimee brought him the coffee every time she travelled to him with the beans harvested in her country, roasted, then packed for export and he had grown to love the particularly bitter flavour. However he was immensely proud of how his role with the family was developing and knew that for every day like today there would be another day where he would be able to stand down and relax, now wasn't the time to think about when. There was a small amount of activity in the port with several yachts being prepared for outings by their crews for later in the day, the day was already starting to warm he thought to himself just as he saw a figure rise from one of the plinths holding statues on the quay and walking towards the steps down to the water where he would moor the small inflatable. At first glance the figure appeared slight, a woman he was sure and as she got closer he could see she appeared to be of European appearance with blonde hair, dressed business like with a small case and a pack over her shoulder. She descended easily down the steps and as she reached his level he realised he was looking straight in to the eyes of Mariam who he had least seen in Cairo.

During the 15 minutes it took them to return to the Dianawa in the inflatable, Mariam filled him in on the details since their meeting in Cairo, after Chris had reported back relatively favourably Kahil had made her an offer she could not refuse although initially she had before they eventually wore her down and it became a matter of when she would re-join the family not if. Mariam definitely fascinated Chris and despite his love for Aimee he was always comfortable in her company and he knew her time on the Dianawa would mean he had a dependable colleague he could trust over what promised to be a challenging few days with the guests on board. Chris secured the tender and they both headed up to the bridge where the skipper was viewing his charts for the day, he introduced Mariam to the skipper and by his slightly startled reaction he realised that like himself the skipper too thought that Mariam, with her newly bleached hair, paid more than a passing resemblance to Princess Diana, the Princess of Wales.

The Dianawa lifted its anchor and headed roughly East along the coast towards Cannes and Nice and Chris headed to the meeting room on the yacht to plan his security briefing at 5am. Whilst they would pass close to Cannes and Nice Chris had already instructed the skipper that Dada would likely want to stay clear of these large resorts so a course was plotted between 2-3 miles off the coast for the period of the day. During the security briefing Chris reiterated the need for loyalty to the family and the measures they would all be following until the end of the voyage. The skipper confirmed that the Dianawa had the capacity to stay at sea for several weeks if necessary and could easily outrun most attempts from the media to catch them, the main concern from the meeting had been their ability to be tracked and listened to on their mobile phones with most of the crew having a device of some kind and the agreement had been to stay out of range of the shore based phone masts.

Chris returned to his cabin where he sat at his small desk working out a short briefing for when he was able to grab time with Dada, he handled the pressure very well and rather than worry about what lay ahead he saw every day as a learning opportunity. Those close to him said he lacked emotion never getting angry or ever getting over excited but he left it to the jury as to whether this was a good or a bad thing. He had just finished preparing his brief and was shaving when the skipper radioed to say Dada had been on the bridge and had asked if Chris could be on deck for a breakfast meeting at 8.30am to discuss the day's arrangements.

Chris finished shaving and pulled on the family's preferred tan uniform before heading out on to deck, as he passed his wardrobe he winked in to the full length mirror and smiled at what he saw looking back at him, he was a modest guy but he admitted to himself he had never been in better shape.

He found Dada but to his surprise sat next to him was the Princess, dressed modestly with her hair waving in the breeze and she smiled shyly, almost in a flirting way as Chris approached backing off Dada slightly so the two of them could continue their conversation. Dada approved the day's arrangements and thanked Chris for all his work, a further sign that the respect was growing between them and it hadn't escaped Chris that the younger Kahil was definitely calling the shots on this trip. Dada explained that the latest passenger, Mariam, would effectively be personal assistant to the Princess whilst on board but they were to work closely in ensuring all arrangements off shore or onshore went as smoothly as possible with the minimal intrusion. Chris heard the door from the staff quarters on the deck below open and shortly after Miriam appeared dressed in the company uniform and headscarf and came towards the impromptu meeting on deck, Dada stood and greeted her in the traditional way before stepping back and allowing both the Princess and Mariam to meet for the first time. In the short time Chris had observed the Princess he had found her to be an incredibly humble and almost shy person and in this moment she again showed those qualities by standing up and smiling at Mariam, as Mariam removed her headscarf the Princess initially looked shocked, even paling, but recovered with a small smile and kissed her new assistant on both cheeks. Chris himself was speechless as apart from the slight difference in height, this English Princess and Egyptian employee could have been twins.

For what seemed like an eternity but in reality was a few seconds there was quiet with just the purring of Dianawa's engines the only backdrop of noise as she pulled out of the bay and to sea, then the Princess laughed loudly calling out "More Tea anyone" and everyone relaxed, sat down and started to discuss the days itinerary.

Chapter 14   August 1997 Walworth Road London

The Labour Party headquarters was an old red brick building at the top of the Walworth Road just behind the Elephant and Castle shopping centre which is built beside a labyrinth of roads, subways, footpaths above a busy underground railway intersection. The whole area was a little run down with a mixture of Victorian and 1960's architecture dominating the landscapes often sitting uncomfortably together. A number 12 traditional red bus brought you direct from Westminster and the Houses of Parliament in only 10 minutes which meant Pete could travel between his research office and the party headquarters regularly and he felt that politics was a business where you definitely needed to be seen and his day to day work blended well with the special project he was involved in meaning his face was well known to even the most senior players in the party. Party HQ was an exciting place to be at the moment with them very much being a party in waiting to govern the country. All the leading polls that predicted the outcome of this weeks general election were pointing to a labour landslide and the PM in waiting epitomised the youthful and exuberant feel around the party at the moment. It also felt like a period of modernisation with the stuffy Westminster feel gone and replaced by first name terms, open neck shirts and no ties. But it did mean some long hours and today had been no exception with a 7am start at Westminster and the meeting here at party HQ not due to finish until around 9pm. There was also a social set who often drank together too after work so on some occasions he had found himself rolling in from work after midnight and grabbing 5 hours sleep before the alarm rang again in the morning. Pete was still living in South East London so fortunately could be to and from the offices often in 30 minutes depending on the time of the day but the work had taken a toll on his social life and he had drifted from some of the friends he had made in the capital.

Pete ran through his notes one last time prior to the meeting which would be chaired by the party leader Gordon who had become known amongst his staff as PMIW short for Prime Minister In Waiting. He had presented to him before but on less serious matters, whereas tonight he felt he was presenting a problem without a solution and was thus unsure as to how he may react. Pete had been focussed on security matters when he had stumbled on the issues relating to the Royal Family and was now being seen by the party as somewhat of a Royal expert too. The party was seen as anti-royal as Gordon had been critical of the cost of maintaining the Royal Household and in particular the behaviour of some of the Royals who, in his view, spent too much time in St Moritz and too little time amongst their own people. This played as a strength amongst some traditional labour voters but to ensure the centre ground between the two parties came over to vote Labour he had needed to temper some of his opinions. Prince Charles and the Princess of Wales had caused the current serving government a number of issues throughout the last few years with them both enjoying extra marital relationships before separating in the early 90's, in particular the Princess was said to have very cleverly played the press and the public gaining much sympathy and showing the Royal establishment to be set in its ways, slow to change and very much closing ranks against her. It was Gordon's belief that he could help the Royal Family improve their PR and engineer a peace deal between the Prince and the Princess thus helping them whilst making sure he kept as many of the voters as possible happy too. The 90's had been a difficult period for the Royals but Gordon firmly believed the 00's could be better if they modernised and put themselves at the centre of "New Britain".

The meeting started slightly late as the PMIW had hosted an impromptu press conference when he had arrived at party HQ, he was an enigmatic and believable speaker and the press lapped up the new style and panache that he brought to proceedings, the estimated poll ratings were so positive in his favour that everyone from world leaders to the press were trying to cosy up to him, if those polls right he would be the new British PM within 48 hours. The slight delay made things worse for Pete who was becoming more nervous by the minute but he knew inside that he had nothing to worry about and no-one was here to trip him up.

Gordon kicked off the meeting with a brief overview of what he was hoping to get from the meeting and asked all to be as open and honest as possible, the PMIW hated unnecessary small talk and in coded language had encouraged all the party staff to be as open and honest as possible as part of his wish to bring a new style of politics to the country. Pete had shared a briefing note in advance of the meeting and he was surprised that the PMIW had obviously read it from start to finish. The note had set out general facts and opinions about the Royal Family and how they were currently perceived and indeed how they perceived the PMIW, whilst the Queen stayed neutral without exception it hadn't been unknown for junior Royals to let their feelings known about the PMIW.

Rather than being bothered about the findings Gordon congratulated Pete for not hiding from the difficult questions but then shocked Pete and all those present by saying he had been left believing the briefing note wanted to say something else, as he finished the sentence he turned and looked at Pete and without any change in expression or tone asked Pete "what do you want to tell us that the briefing note didn't say Pete?" Pete was inwardly quite shocked but as was his way he managed to control and mask his feelings before nodding towards the PMIW and saying "in any other environment what I am about to say would be classed as Top Secret, I don't think even the Government are aware of some of the issues I'm about to suggest and this could create the biggest scandal since Profumo, on that basis would you still like me to proceed?"

The PMIW took back control of the meeting and nodded courteously at Pete, he then addressed everyone in the room in saying that the party could not allow anything to divert them from their path to victory so he expected 100% confidentiality from everyone. Everyone murmured their assent and Pete slowly realised everyone in the room was focussed on him so he bought himself some time by taking a sip of water and theatrically wiping his lips before addressing those present.

Pete explained that the Princess of Wales was now in the South of France and, as far as he knew, aboard a yacht belonging to the Kahil family who were significant donors to the Labour Party, some in the room were becoming a little impatient and it was pointed out that this had been headlines in one of the daily papers that morning so was hardly ground breaking news? But Pete plugged on and listed several high profile names that he could evidence the Princess had been known to have close relations with, there was surprise around the room as the names tumbled out but painstakingly Pete was able to evidence each case through his significant research. Whilst not showing impatience the PMIW knew he had another meeting to get to and nodded firmly at Pete that he should reach his conclusion, Pete looked round the room one last time before telling those present "Diana Princess of Wales is in a relationship with Dada Kahil who effectively runs the Kahil business empire on behalf of the family, we understand she may also be several months pregnant and planning to become engaged within in the next week, one of the first issues we will need to deal with in our dealings with the Royal family will be them wanting to prevent the birth of a royal Muslim baby, there is no way the establishment will let this happen". Pete leant back in his chair realising he was wet under the armpits where he had sweated nervously and looked round the room again and said "questions", everyone stared at him, in some cases jaws apart but there was just silence apart from the hum of the traffic outside on the Walworth Road.

Chapter 15   August 1997 South London

Although the gravity of the meeting had been significant it had lasted less than 30 minutes and he was somewhat relieved when he was dismissed but told to report back to the same venue at 10am the following day when a task group would be put together to support the approach the party would need to take. Pete realised he hadn't eaten all day but also felt like he needed a stiff drink, he decided not to head back towards Westminster and instead cut through the sprawling Heygate estate on to the New Kent Road where he purchased a kebab before boarding a 53 bus down the Old Kent Road to New Cross, he knew he should really have an early night but he also needed to relax so he jumped off the bus at New Cross and went in the Rose pub which on weekday nights played his favourite cheesy 80's pop music. A few of the regulars recognised him and he was soon deep in conversation which drifted between politics, football and the local music scene. Pete was often vague about his job and people didn't question him too much, he didn't mind this as he liked the separation between "home" and "work". He also enjoyed drinks with work colleagues but felt he had to act differently, he couldn't be himself in a lot of ways and was more guarded about his private life. Over the last few years he had been much more open about his sexuality but change was happening slowly and Pete didn't want to jeopardise his career through careless talk. At the Rose it was a mixed crowd, he was always comfortable there and had even been known to occasionally dance on the bar and sing on the karaoke, the pub really had three trades, during the day older locals would sit and watch the racing or other sport taking their time over a pint or two whilst later in the afternoon a commuting crowd would come in for a couple of drinks on their way home, a perfect venue being just a stone's throw from New Cross railway station. Later in the evening it was generally a younger crown, mainly gay but not exclusively so and things could get a bit more raucous but always respectful. However, Pete knew if he was to progress within the party he needed to think about his behaviour, where he socialised and with whom. When Gordon the PMIW had spoken at the recent party conference he had told members to go away and prepare for Government, this included behaving in the right manner, particularly important as they had campaigned on an anti-sleaze platform after the scandal hit tory years of the early 90's. Party members and employees had been asked to sign up to a code of conduct and also confirm there was nothing in their past that could haunt them in the future.

Pete left the pub feeling a little tipsy, although he had eaten it must have been the adrenalin of the meeting followed by several quick drinks that had lightened his head, the streets were busy despite the time and the sound of loud music came from several houses as people took advantage of the warm weather to party in their gardens. As he walked away from the pub two guys refused to yield out of the way and barged him in to the wall of the pub glaring at him as they walked on, Pete was slightly shaken but by the time he straightened himself up they were long gone in to the distance. He put his wallet in deep into his front pocket and carried on reaching home and saw there had been a call from Dave, in the communal area there was a payphone and incoming messages were scrawled on a board above and he made a mental note to call him back at a more reasonable time the following day.

Pete woke the following morning to the sound of the communal payphone ringing in the hallway, he reached around himself and discovered he was still fully clothed and had fallen asleep on top of the bed, he had a slight hangover, a sore shoulder and his breath tasted of stale ale and spices from last night's takeaway, he checked his watch and realised he had overslept and he was due back at party HQ in 90 minutes. Whilst this was possible even after showering and shaving it would give him little time to prepare for the follow up meeting on the royal issues, he put on the kettle and popped some toast and put on the radio which led with two main stories namely the forthcoming elections and the Princess of Wales and her latest overseas trip, how ironic thought Pete.

As he left his flat he realised that he hadn't called Dave back, it wasn't like Dave to have called twice so close together but he also couldn't afford to be late for the follow up meeting with the PMIW so instead he headed down the street and on to the main A2 road which came in from the Kent area, from here he could get a bus almost to the front door of party headquarters. He boarded the bus showing his season ticket to the driver who barely acknowledged his existence sat behind his plastic screen in the cab, luckily the bus was able to use a dedicated bus lane for most of the journey through the South London suburbs and he actually arrived in his workplace 30 minutes before the meeting was due to start. He used one of the shared desks to set out all his notes and make sure that anything he was asked, he could answer consistently with the briefing he had done the previous night. His stock was rising in the party HQ and many realised he potentially had a great career ahead of him, subsequently people would stop off and talk to him asking what he was working on, it hadn't gone unnoticed that the previous evening he had briefed Gordon, the PMIW, and people were fascinated as to the reasons, Pete also realised that idle gossip would get him nowhere but had developed a perfect way of batting away the questions without people feeling he was being dismissive.

The meeting with Gordon and his staff was disappointingly short for Pete and he was asked few questions about what he had presented the previous evening. Instead the PMIW outlined that he was setting up a task force to work on the issues they had discussed but that the task force would work discretely and report only to the PMIW and his chief of staff. Given the potential gravity of the matter the PMIW had appointed a senior member of the party's communications group, Mike Ansell, to lead the work. Mike was well liked in the party and respected as someone previously responsible for communications for the secret government agency MI6, he had significant experience of dealing with the Royal Family too so Pete could see he would be a good fit.

Chapter 16   At sea on the Dianawa

Chris had been surprised at the change of plan even though the press intrusion had gotten worse. Over the last few days, they had been able to see journalists on the shore via their high powered binoculars and there had been two occasions where helicopters had flown low over the Dianawa. Whilst they had been spotted in advance and the passengers had all disappeared below deck, the intrusion was starting to frustrate Dada and also put strain on Chris's team who were permanently on look out duty. Things had come to a head the previous evening when Dada had asked the captain to change course and head for Carteret, a small seaside resort and port situated on the Contentinental peninsular of Normandy. The Port of Carteret itself is sometimes called a "port of the isles", ferry services have run from here to the channel islands since the latter part of the 19th century, the small port around 40km south of Cherbourg was enlarged with the help of combat engineers from the American 280th Battalion stationed in Carteret in 1945 and used to a limited extent in the D-day landings. From the South of France it would have been a considerable journey by road but given the geography of France it was going to be an even longer journey by sea as they first headed south passing the Balearic islands then heading through the strait of Gibraltar in to the Atlantic and then across the Bay of Biscay towards Carteret. Chris had been up on the bridge and the captain was estimating a journey time of around 45 hours as long as the Kahil family didn't insist on any impromptu stops en route. For this reason the captain had stayed clear of Majorca, Minorca and Ibiza plotting a course to the East of these popular holiday destination islands and shortly they would turn slightly west and head for the narrow straight between Spain and North Africa. The mood on board was more relaxed, the passengers were openly wandering around on deck without fear of being spotted and the radar showed an array of commercial traffic, ferries, container ships and tankers which you would expect to see in these busy waters.

Chris had been asked to prepare for a low key arrival at the Port of Carteret but to make transport available for the family to travel together onwards to Paris by road once they had disembarked. This suited Chris as he had looked at the options to get the family helicopter in and the closest airfield was the aerodrome at nearby Granville, however this itself was heavily used at this time of year by tourists from the UK who could fly over from the south of England in less than an hour. The plan was therefore to have two large mini vans to take the family and limited amount of staff to Paris and Mariam was arranging for luggage and equipment to be ready for them when they arrived in Paris. The Dianawa would only be booked in to the port at the last moment and instead had been booked to arrive in to Poole on the south coast of England, if anyone did happen to be tracking their movements the course they were following supported this and wouldn't raise suspicion.

The following morning Dada asked if they could call in to Gibraltar as a fellow alumni from his old school lived there and he was keen to discuss business opportunities. Chris had agreed it was a logical place to stop between the South of France and the UK so hadn't objected, nothing about their arrival there would give anyone watching a hint that they were actually headed for Normandy in France. Gibraltar is a British Overseas Territory and city located at the southern tip of the Iberian Peninsula. It has an area of only 2.6 sq miles and is bordered to the north by Spain. The landscape is dominated by the Rock of Gibraltar, at the foot of which is a densely populated town area, home to some 30,000 people, primarily Gibraltarians. They arrived in port barely noticed as this was a busy stop off point for commercial vessels from all over the world as well as being used by the UK navy. Al Kahil sensed a future business opportunity given its unique location close to North Africa, Spain and Portugal and after a productive meeting with his old friend they were back out to sea, they had stopped for such a short time the Princess hadn't even left her cabin which, Chris mused, was probably a good thing in a town that seemed to be more British than anywhere in Britain.
Mariam and Chris grabbed dinner together as the Dianawa left port and headed back out towards the Atlantic, Mariam appeared a little stressed by the

change of plan and the logistics she now needed to organise but Chris was sure she would take it all in her stride. Since they had entered the Atlantic things were quiet on board, as impressive a vessel the Dianawa was, she was definitely being thrown around in the rough Atlantic seas and this was likely to continue as they headed across the notoriously fickle Bay of Biscay.

Mariam filled Chris in on her time with the Princess and indeed marvelled at what a down to earth person she was to work with, they talked about strategies to keep their employers and guests safe once they got to France as they were both sure at some point there was going to be a media frenzy as the worlds press tried to snap the people's princess with the multi-millionaire playboy.

Five Days before, Heysham Lancashire UK

John was in the companies dockside office at Heysham, it was a typical blustery day at the harbour with the winds that blew across the entrance making docking so difficult at times. His boss was clearly pleased with the progress John was making and had even talked about him being the youngest captain on the fleet in living memory if things kept going in the right direction.
As part of his development he was now being asked if he would move across to one of the freight ships which was to fulfil a special charter to the Channel Islands

before returning north some time the following week, the only catch being he would have to leave within twenty four hours. This seemed like a great opportunity to both further his development and see some of the British Isles and North Coast of France at the same time and gain experience in other waters. The dilemma was he was due to be on leave and had various things booked but as he played the options through in his mind he was reminded of the words of one of his old teachers and decided to "grasp the moment".

So forty eight hours later he found himself on the freighter the Manx Maid on a night watch heading down the Irish Sea where they would eventually head around Lands End and cross directly to the Channel Islands, little did he know that his old school friend Chris was at the same time heading across the Bay of Biscay on the Dianawa towards Normandy.

Chapter 17   Arriving at Carteret

The last part of the voyage had been quiet as they had reached more sheltered areas after passing through the Bay of Biscay, Chris was on the bridge with Mariam having an early morning coffee as at first the coast and then the harbour of Carteret came in to view. It was a calm but misty morning and at this hour the only movement on the sea were the fishing trawlers returning with their catch which within a few hours would be available to purchase on the quayside or packed and distributed across the rest of the country. Chris and Miriam were unsure when they would see each other again as once the family reached Paris it was likely they would all go their separate ways and subsequently the staff too. Chris looked across at Mariam not for the first time that morning and thought to himself how like the Princess she was in size, stature and looks with really only her slightly darker complexion being a real distinguishing feature. They had reduced down to around 5 knots as they followed the channel in, although the skipper was extremely experienced, this was not an area of coastline he was familiar with and "the Dianawa was an expensive toy to damage", he had joked with Chris. All looked quiet ahead so Chris took the opportunity to check again the plans for the day and the various arrangements he had made. Whilst they would dock before 6am Kahil had asked for the onward transport to arrive no earlier than 9am allowing them a last breakfast aboard the luxury yacht. The plan was for one vehicle to go ahead with the luggage first, Mariam would be aboard this one and as well as ensuring there wasn't a build up of vehicles around the yacht it meant that she could get to Paris earlier and begin to supervise the unpacking of the families belongings and ensure she was ready for the functions they would be attending that evening. A second vehicle would leave shortly after with support staff before the family themselves left around an hour later. As far as the worlds media were concerned the Dianawa had vanished off the face of the earth, unknown to Chris various stories had been run across the media with guesses as wild as North Africa, the Greek Islands and even crossing the Atlantic to the US, whilst the Dianawa was indeed capable of any of these it looked like the family had dodged the media well and the media had not anticipated this circuitous route back to the north of France.

The Dianawa finally tied up alongside the quay at Carteret and it wouldn't take long for word to get out far and wide that the family and their special guest were back on dry land, Chris was certain that this would intensify as they were almost certainly tracked on their way up to Paris, as inconspicuous as they were trying to be someone somewhere would spot them and the media watchers in Paris would also be stationed at all the families usual haunts.

One of those haunts was The Paris Ritz (which the family owned) where Dada kept a Penthouse suite at his disposal and this is where the family would now head along with the Princess of Wales. The Ritz overlooks the Place Vendôme in the city's 1st arrondissement and is ranked among the most luxurious hotels in the world.

The hotel had been founded in 1898 by the Swiss hotelier César Ritz in collaboration with the French chef Auguste Escoffier and constructed behind the façade of an eighteenth-century townhouse. It was among the first hotels in Europe to provide an en-suite bathroom, electricity, and a telephone for each room. It had quickly established a reputation for luxury and attracted a clientele that included royalty, politicians, writers, film stars, and singers as well as the super rich like the Kahil family themselves. Indeed several of its suites have been named in honour of famous guests of the hotel including Coco Chanel, and the cocktail lounge Bar Hemingway pays tribute to the famous writer Ernest Hemingway.

Paul Bernard acted as the families security and driver in Paris and the Kahil family had been happy with this arrangement for many years, however the Princess took security needs to a whole different level and Chris had tried, but failed, to convince Dada that he should have oversight of security in Paris as well but had so far been unsuccessful. He had only met Bernard a handful of times but Chris's impression had been of an ill disciplined man who drank too much, Chris himself would not dream of drinking on duty or indeed during the 24 hours before. As well as potentially affecting his performance he thought it set a bad example to the rest of the crew. At around 9am Bernard arrived and Dada and the Princess of Wales got in to the Mercedes and the car sped off initially towards Caen and then across to the A15 autoroute and Paris. By the time they arrived at The Ritz in Paris several hours later they were being followed by several cars and motorbikes with paparazzi reporters trying to get pictures to go with the breaking story that Diana Princess of Wales had arrived in Paris.

As much as Chris didn't rate Bernard it had to be said that he had done a good job in protecting the Princesses' privacy on arrival. They arrived at the rear entrance where Mariam was waiting and took Dada and the Princess directly to the top floor and the Penthouse suite where items had already been unpacked awaiting their arrival. That evening they planned to have dinner but first the Princess wanted to take advantage of the hotel's swimming pool, the largest indoor pool in Paris which had been kept closed off to other guests for such an eventuality. Following the swim she had asked for time to rest so Mariam had retreated and took a little time herself to reflect on a whirlwind few days.

During the morning Chris had been told to be in the Hemingway bar in the Ritz for 8pm as he would be expected to accompany Dada, the Princess and Bernard as they headed off to the restaurant, Chris felt somewhat vindicated that his presence had been requested although a little blindsided that he wasn't fully aware of arrangements. On arrival at the rear entrance of the Ritz Chris had had strong words with Bernard who was openly in discussion with a number of the journalists hovering around the hotel area, indeed Chris was pretty certain that Bernard and/or the hotel staff had tipped them off about the Royal presence, but with time ticking away he had left to ensure he was in the bar area on time. As Dada and the Princess entered the bar there was an audible collective gasp from customers followed by disappointment when they left with Chris through the side door and to the waiting Mercedes with Bernard at the wheel.

Chris held the door for the Princess as she got in the car, it was his first glance of her, as in the bar area and whilst exiting the hotel his stare had been fixed on the surroundings, movements and any potential threats, his jaw must have visibly dropped as he got an almost nervous laugh back at him by return and before he could say anything Bernard yelled at him to get in the passenger seat before flooring the accelerator and racing in to the early evening traffic on Rue Cambon. After leaving the Rue Cambon and crossing the Place de la Concorde, they drove along Cours la Reine and Cours Albert 1er, the embankment road along the right bank of the River Seine and into the Place de l'Alma underpass.

It had been obvious almost immediately that they were being followed by a variety of small cars and motorcycles and Bernard seemed almost thrilled by the prospect of a chase, indeed he was reaching such breakneck speeds Chris made the decision to fasten his seatbelt keeping one hand close to the release button should he need to exit quickly. Via the rear view mirror he noted Dada had done the same just before they entered the Pont de l'Alma tunnel which ran parallel with the river Seine. As they entered the tunnel things suddenly happened very quickly and Chris noted particularly the erratic behaviour of the paparazzi chasing the car before glancing at the speedometer which showed a speed of 65k/m/h more than twice the legal limit for this stretch of road. Bernard seemed to have lost control of the car and at that point they glanced against a smaller white car and swerved to the left of the two-lane carriageway and colliding head-on with a supporting roof pillar. The car then spun and hit the wall of the tunnel backwards finally coming to a stop with substantial damage, particularly to the front half of the vehicle.

The photographers had been driving behind the Mercedes and when they reached the scene, some rushed to help, trying to open the doors and help the victims, while some of them took pictures, Chris had suffered facial injuries and was concussed but afterwards clearly remembered looking across at the driver Bernard who was obviously dead and recalled seeing a hand hold his neck down, inject him before he himself felt a sharp sting and then only blackness. The first Police officers arrived around ten minutes after the crash and found Bernard slumped forward and deceased in the driver's seat and one passengers in the back of the vehicle directly behind the driver unrecognisable due to their injuries, neither had been wearing seatbelts, in the front it was noted that the air bags had functioned in the front and rear passenger side but not on the driver's side, the passenger doors on the right hand side of the car were open and there was no one in the front or rear seats on the right hand side.

45 minutes after the crash a helicopter lifted from Le Bourget airport 8 miles north east of the crash scene and headed north west in the direction of Normandy.

Chapter 18   A week that shook the world

<u>Sunday 3am Ripon North Yorkshire</u>

Prime Minister Gordon Barnes was dreaming about bells ringing when he suddenly woke and realised that the bell ringing was the red phone that had been installed in his constituency office in Ripon North Yorkshire, this meant that it would be an extremely urgent message and as he looked at his wrist and saw it was 2am he pondered that indeed this was not likely to be good news. He shook himself together and when he looked back at this moment some weeks later he thought how bizarre that a national emergency started with him climbing out of bed wearing very little, the family dog bounding up to him and finding his teenage son sat in the kitchen worse for wear after a late night out.

It was his private secretary on the phone who wanted to patch through the British Ambassador in Paris who had tried but failed to reach the foreign secretary, his first port of call. After brief pleasantries the ambassador had cut in and shared the news that Diana, Princess of Wales, had been involved in a horrific car accident and at this stage it was possible that although still alive she may not pull through. As he walked back through the house to his bedroom and his wife stirred in their bed, he thought to himself how he had prepared for so many things on becoming Prime Minister but he had not prepared for this. As he started to crystalize a plan in his mind his son walked through with possibly the worst cup of coffee he had ever tasted, and he smiled grimly to himself and knew that it was for moments like this he had aspired to the position.

Sunday 9am Ripon North Yorkshire

The last 6 hours had somehow flown by whilst at the same time it had felt like he was in a slow-motion dream, his private secretary had dashed up the A1 in four hours to be with him and he had just been briefed by his media team. In the past 6 hours he had made calls to the French President, Prince Charles and the Queen's private secretary as well as giving the order to hold an emergency cabinet meeting to discuss the crisis that was unfolding. Now he walked out to face the media already camped on his doorstep to who he spoke without taking questions announcing the death of the Princess of Wales. As he went back into his kitchen after the media appearance and took his third strong coffee of the day his private secretary told him he had absolutely nailed it 100% and whilst that sounded so wrong in the situation, he knew he was absolutely right too.

Sunday 11am Ripon North Yorkshire

Ripon Racecourse lay just a mile south of the city in beautiful green surroundings, he had made a very brief appearance here yesterday amongst the regions racegoers and had been cheered as, ironically, he had walked into the winners enclosure for photographs with a successful local racehorse owner. The media had reacted positively to this which played in to his "man of the people" image but he had hardly expected to be back here less than 24 hours later and even less expected to be climbing up in to a military helicopter and en route back to Downing Street, however he was determined that this government was seen to be in control of issues and that he personally led from the front and as this was the first test of this policy it was right that he would make the 50 minute flight back down to London and just before Midday he was on the ground at Parliament Square where a black Range Rover was waiting for him taking him the short distance to Downing Street as the bell of big ben tolled every minute announcing to the nation the death of the Princess.

Sunday 2pm Cabinet Office Room A Whitehall

The PM looked around the room at the assembled ministers and senior civil servants, they were a good team handpicked by Gordon himself but whilst he had picked them for their particular skills the stares he got back were of some trepidation, like himself none of them expected to be in this position so new in to their roles and the first some of them had been aware were either by the media briefing he himself had given or urgent calls from staffers desperately trying to track down ministers who had returned to constituencies and family homes for the weekend. Those assembled were briefed by the PM and foreign secretary before opening to questions of which there were few. Each minister was given a clear responsibility and asked to report back at a further briefing that would be held at 3pm that afternoon in the same room, responsibilities ranged from liaison with the media, military, religious organisations, royal family and various authorities to organisations that would now be brought in to provide logistical support to the largest funeral since the death of Winston Churchill

Sunday 5pm Downing Street

Pete had had a late night the previous evening as he had been invited to a party close to his home, he had half woken up with a smile on his face until he realised he could hear the National Anthem being played on a TV somewhere in the vicinity, he had immediately put his own TV on to see the news that the UK was waking up to and as things developed in front of him he found breathing became more difficult, the colour drained from his face, his legs were shaking and he realised he was in the middle of a panic attack, all the data he had gathered was correct.

Since the party had entered government he had embraced his role as special advisor on constitutional matters but had seen very little of the Prime Minister now sat in front of him, for the first time since taking power Gordon looked worn out and stressed but when he spoke it was with that assertiveness Pete was used to. Gordon asked Pete for a list of people who were aware of the work he had done on the Royal Family and in particular the information he had gained on the Princess of Wales and her new lover. Pete swallowed and weakly told Gordon that he couldn't reveal his sources but knew this denial would be futile, however he was shaken by what happened next. Gordon reached in to his desk drawer and took out an envelope, from the envelope he took out a photo which he passed to Pete, as Pete studied it for the second time that day his legs shook and he was almost physically sick when he saw an eight year old picture of himself firstly leaving the casino with a 1980's rock star then a second picture taken through a window of him knelt in front of the same rock star who had his trousers round his ankles. Gordon smiled thinly at him and Pete wrote down Dave's name and address up in the Shetland Islands.

<u>Monday 6pm St Peter Port Guernsey</u>

John was on the bridge of the Manx Maid preparing the ship for departure later that evening under the watchful of the captain, it had been a very busy day overseeing the loading of various containers for their client who had chartered the ship prior to departure back to the Isle of Man. The journey back would take around 30 hours across to the UK coast, around Lands' End and up through the Irish Sea back to their home port of Douglas.

The previous day John had managed some time off and had explored the principal town of the island, St Peters Port, and also a circuit of the island by bus. The port itself was busy with a mixture of pleasure craft, ferries, fishing boats and small yachts, as he had stood on the bridge watching the sunset he had seen a sleek private yacht arrive in port and envied at whoever had the money to own and operate such a vessel.
Guernsey is the second largest island in the Channel Islands and is located 27 miles west of the Cotentin Peninsula, Normandy. The island has a population of around 60,000 people and the island has a land area of only 24 square miles, however John realised it has some of the richest people in the world living in that small area.

Guernsey is administered as part of the Bailiwick of Guernsey, a self-governing dependency of the British Crown. The island is therefore not part of the United Kingdom, although the UK government has certain responsibilities for the dependency. The British monarch is the head of state though and wherever John had been that day the talk had been about the death of Diana Princess of Wales, it was made all the more poignant as a number of senior people on the island were suggesting she had been due to visit the dependency that Autumn.

Eventually the Manx Maid was ready for sea and he was informed by the crew that all doors were sealed and ready for departure. John still knew little about the cargo they had been chartered to carry although the little he did understand was that it could be the final shipment from the family he had spoken to Colin about who were relocating to the island.

He had enjoyed his time on the Manx Maid and the experience of another vessel; however, it would be the local pilot who took them out to sea before being dropped off in to a fast launch as they turned and made a course for home. John lapped up the information the harbour pilot was sharing not taking too much notice of surroundings as the ropes were loosened, the capstans reeled in the slack and the Manx Maid headed out of the harbour. As they passed the end of the harbour wall though John looked across at the private yacht still tied up where it had berthed last night, he saw a figure walking down the starboard side of the vessel, his purpose and stance unmistakenly someone who had served in the military, the man was wearing a cap and sunglasses but both the purpose with which he moved and his shape were in some way familiar to John, something that continued to puzzle him for most of the journey home.

Tuesday 9am Bressay Shetlands

Dave was out on his morning exercise down towards the bottom end of the island and the lighthouse, at the part of the road where it came closest to the sea he was sure he had heard the outdoor motor of a fast moving dinghy but he couldn't see anything, it was a particularly windy day and he saw the ferry arriving from Aberdeen which must have been delayed due to the rough weather. He thought to himself he had maybe been mistaken and set off again. He saw the Post Office Van in the distance turn into a farm track, it had come over from Lerwick to deliver to the small number of residents on the island and Dave waved but today the driver mustn't have seen him as it carried on with no acknowledgment. It was the last thing he saw as seconds later something hit him in the back of the head, and he fell forward in to the road with his wheelchair falling on top of him.

Saturday 10pm – Downing Street London

Gordon sat back in his office and thought briefly about the people who had sat there before him and the decisions they had had to make. The funeral of Diana had been a moment where the nation had stopped and come together, he had welcomed world leaders, some of the most powerful in the world both prior to and after the ceremony, less than a week before he could not have imagined how the week would turn out but as he sipped his drink he smiled and with the public turning against the Royal Family after their ambivalent response to Diana's death Gordon had come out very well indeed, even newspapers that generally supported the opposition parties were describing him as a true leader, it had been an incredible week, but for Gordon a very positive one.

<u>Sunday 8am Cairo Egypt</u>

Mohammed held his wife in his arms as they sat in front of their apartment in the suburbs of Cairo close to Giza. They had moved here to be nearer to their work and Mariam had purchased the property for them with the money she had made from her new work. Mohammed was disappointed in Mariam at times and the way she had rejected her religion in his eyes and the western habits she seemed to have gained but without question he loved his daughter. They often sat here to watch the sun rise, particularly on a Sunday when neither of them worked, however it had now been almost three weeks since they had heard from Mariam and as his wife had reminded him for the umpteenth time this had never happened before, not even for a week. Whilst he comforted his wife and said all the correct positive things, as he watched the sun rise into its position high in the Egyptian summer sky, deep inside him his heart was saying Mariam was gone forever.

Sunday 1pm Ronaldsway Airport, Isle of Man

Chris was waiting at the small airport, the only passenger airport on the Isle of man and for the first time in a week his heart skipped and he smiled as he saw her walking down the steps in that special way she held herself, the flight had come in from Heathrow as she had connected there on her long haul journey in to the UK.

Chris still hadn't rationalised the last week and the awful events of the previous weekend when the family had been thrust into the limelight with the death of Dada and Diana. It was only now he realised that he may have been a small pawn in a giant game and someone else had been pulling the strings all along. He had not managed to obtain any answers from the Kalil family who were bound in their own grief for the loss of their son who, according to tradition, had been buried within 48 hours of the terrible accident.

There were too many questions he couldn't answer and even more he hadn't been able to ask. What had happened to Mariam? How had he got back to the Dianawa? What had he seen being loaded on to the ship he had seen in Guernsey and was that really his old friend John that he had seen on the bridge of the freighter as it had left port?

Despite all this he had that familiar warm feeling as Aimee reached the bottom of the steps, even though she had been travelling for 14 hours she looked business like, smart, perfectly dressed and so elegant and as she saw him waiting her beaming smile overcame all the tiredness in his body, as she reached him they embraced for what seemed like minutes as he ran his hands up and down her body, something good had come from this week after all.

Chapter 19   March 2022 North Yorkshire

Adnan boarded the bus from York to Leeds, he was escaping the boarding school which had been his home for seven years for the day to be with like-minded friends in Leeds. As the bus joined the A64 and headed west towards Leeds he reflected on the education he was receiving, after five years as a model secondary pupil he was now almost at the end of his two years as a 6th former, this included certain privileges like being able to spend the day outside of school at the weekend as long as you returned by 9pm. He was 24 and around 6 years older than most of his year group, for family reasons he had been kept out of the education system in his early years but with his un-remarkable stature and baby face looks even the other students closest to him had no idea about the age gap.

Life at the school had been mixed, he realised he came from a very privileged background which afforded the annual fees, but he didn't respect his parents for sending him to the school as it seemed to Adnan that they just wanted him out of the way. Both his parents lived as recluses on a huge estate with little or no contact with the outside world, this had made Adnan insular himself and he had found it hard to mix with people when he first joined the school. With mixed parentage he neither felt part of the "traditional" white British cohort or part of those from different ethnic groups and in fact both groups had tended to pick on him which he had grown to despise.

However, he had joined groups on-line and now had a firm set of friends he talked to most nights, friends that he felt he could trust and who had felt that same sense of isolation as him. They were meeting today in Headingley on the west side of Leeds meaning Adnan was having to catch three buses to make the meeting at Midday. He walked in to the Costa on Otley Road in Headingley and immediately saw his friends and after ordering a coffee he joined them, the shop was full mainly of students from the nearby universities, some of them using the space to revise, and together Adnan and his friends just looked like another group of students discussing their studies or activities over the weekend.

Adnan really looked up to Hussain who was almost the self -styled leader of the group on-line, Hussain was born and bred in Leeds the youngest of four children. His father was of Pakistani origin and worked in a factory, while his mother worked as an interpreter for British Pakistani families at the hospital where Hussain was born despite coming from a middle class white background and never herself visiting Pakistan.

Adnan loved talking to Hussain about football and cricket something they both excelled in although

Hussain had not had the same privileged education, he had achieved great exam results and recently passed a vocational qualification in travel and tourism. This was the fourth consecutive Saturday they had met and when Hussain had suggested visiting his Mosque together with Adnan and his other friends Shehzad and Tanweer, Adnan saw this as a great honour and as he jumped on his fourth bus of the day back towards the centre of Leeds he thought to himself how, for the first time in years he really felt he belonged. Tanweer worked at his father's butchers shop whilst Shehzad was still studying but together they met one of the elders in a room at the back of the mosque and discussed topics ranging from being a Muslim in Britain today through to the situation in countries like Syria, Afghanistan and some of the West African countries that were still struggling to shake off issues left by their past colonial rulers. Unlike at his school he felt he could express how he felt without being ridiculed and his views seemed to be respected and listened to.

Hussain accompanied him back to the bus station at the end of the day and he travelled back via York to the school on the Yorkshire Moors giving him lots of time to think. He really felt he could trust Hussain, Tanweer and Shezad but despite this he still worried how they would react when he told them about his own privileged background. After spending the afternoon at the mosque and passing Hussains house he realised that his upbringing was light years away from their own struggles, could they genuinely form a band of brothers?

Eventually the bus from York dropped him in the village from where he had to walk the final mile back to the school, this was his least favourite part as the local youths tended to hate all the pupils at the school and on a Saturday evening they were sure to be hanging around on the village rec. Sure enough as he approached the jeers started and then one shouted out "oh look a privileged packi" laughing at himself proud of the abuse he was shouting. Adnan thought about turning and telling them in fact his mother was British and his father Egyptian, but he knew he would be wasting his own breath, instead he pulled up his collar and walked purposefully back to school where he just made it for the 9pm curfew. Back in his dormitory he was brought a hot chocolate and then it was lights out, but Adnan couldn't sleep as he reflected on the day, the things he had heard and how he felt part of something for the first time in a long time.

The following week he repeated the journey but this time almost without thinking when he signed out of school, he wrote down that he was travelling to York not Leeds, he didn't want anyone to know about his new friends although he didn't really know why. They again met in the same place before travelling to the Mosque where they focussed mainly on further Islamic studies and the opportunity to travel to achieve this at a Madrasa out in Pakistan.

Tanweer, Shazad and Hussain were travelling to the Lake District National Park in several weeks' time and asked Adnan if he would like to go with them, Adnan's heart almost burst with pride at being invited by his new friends who explained that during the day they would take part in rafting, canoeing, hiking and climbing whilst in the evening they would further their studies. After returning to the school that evening he decided to call his parents spending twenty minutes on the phone explaining the opportunity he had to visit the Lake District, he promised that as it coincided with the schools Easter holidays he would still be able to visit "home" for two weeks. His Mum agreed almost immediately and Adnan reflected afterwards would his parents have minded if he had said he wouldn't be home at all during the holidays? But he kept those thoughts to himself and his Mum said she would ensure there was sufficient money in his account to help with travel and making sure he had a comfortable trip.

During the week Adnan and his friends chatted on-line every time they got chance planning their trip to the Lake District and before he knew it he was at Leeds station meeting Hussain, Tanweer and Shezad for the train over to Lancaster then another train that would take them to the Lake District. The others had been grateful that he had bought the tickets for the train and as they set off Hussain shared some home cooked food and they were soon in Lancaster. An hour later they were at Windermere station where a driver from the Tarn Fell outward bounds centre was waiting for them. Although Adnan had travelled regularly with school it was the first time he had travelled on an unorganised trip and he was struggling to contain his excitement, on one hand he didn't want his friends to be unimpressed but he also wanted to show his enthusiasm. He had already noticed that travelling with a group of Asians attracted attention he hadn't had before, at Lancaster a man, drunk at an unbelievably early hour, had asked Hussein "what's in the rucksack", a clear reference to a terrorist attack some years ago in London. Adnan had wanted to react, but Hussain had gently put his hand on Adnan's arm indicating to him to back down and forget it.

On arrival they checked in to a shared dormitory and after unpacking Adnan sat on the veranda looking over Lake Coniston, it had been one of those typical spring days where one minute it was raining and the next wall to wall sunshine but for now it had turned in to a clear and warm evening. Adnan saw movement to the right and noticed Hussain walking in animated conversation coming from the lake with someone he didn't recognise, they clearly knew each other although it wasn't Shazad or Tanweer, but Adnan didn't care, he was just happy to be here and so happy to belong, he knew with this band of brothers that everything was achievable.

The following morning, they left the Tarn Fell centre early and were taken up to Glenridding towards the north of the Lake District. In the morning they walked the full length of Ullswater which was around 12 miles before regrouping for lunch at the opposite end of the lake. In the afternoon following nothing more than the briefest of briefing sessions they returned to Glenridding in Kayaks arriving back eventually at 4pm. Adnan was fit and at school played rugby weekly as well as participating in martial arts, but nothing had prepared him for the toughness of the day and the need to work together with his friends to propel themselves back to the starting point. At around halfway he had considered quitting, it was a cold windy day and despite being an inland lake the wind blowing up the valley created waves and a strong current against them made life tough. At one point Adnan was convinced they were going backwards but he wouldn't give in and bit by bit they progressed towards their target where they eventually celebrated together. The following days progressed much the same with him feeling like he was being tested to the limit both mentally and physically and he realised that somehow, and he wasn't sure how, they had been brought together as a team for their strengths, different skills and their determination to never ever give up.

On their final day they were taken by Landrover over the Langdales at 3am before dropping down close to Wast Water from where they would climb Scafell Pike the highest mountain in England. Adnan was surprised by his own body, despite being tested beyond what he had ever done before he felt strangely fit and like his new friends, he practically ran up Scafell Pike arriving just after sunrise. Looking towards the coast as the clouds started to break on what turned out to be a beautiful west Lake District morning they first saw the lake below come in to view then Tanweer pointed out Sellafield, the nuclear facility which was an awful blot on the Lake District landscape. As the others focussed on this Adnan was instead drawn to the view opening up across the Irish Sea and he realised that 70 miles to the west he could just make out the outline of Snaefell, the highest point on the Isle of Man where his family home was and where his parents would almost certainly be right now. Deep inside he felt that the circle of life was closing around him, and he looked to the heavens and screamed with delight.

Chapter 20   March 2022 Isle of Man

Just as Adnan had reached the peak of Scafell Pike John was enjoying his regular run along the seafront in Douglas, since relocating to the Isle of Man over ten years ago he had run this route at least once a week from his home in Onchan just above Douglas. He would follow the coastal path and down on to the promenade in Douglas, although the islands capital was relatively sheltered it was not unusual to find himself running one way in to what seemed to be a gale and then turning for home and being blown back along the promenade. If he was out early enough he would see the ferry arriving in from Heysham, it was still timed to arrive at the time that in years gone by it would have brought the Royal Mail and daily newspapers ready for the islands residents, but these days there was less demand for printed media and the mail came in by plane to the small airport just across the Island. However, the Island population very much relied on the ferry still for the fresh produce with priority given on each sailing to retailers who brought across the essentials that would be on the supermarket shelves within hours. The weather today was calm, and his colleague would have had a relatively easy crossing although it looked like there had been a mist sat on the sea which would have made visibility harder. By the time he arrived home the ferry had already docked and was unloading and he showered and dressed before his wife Trudy brought him tea and toast and they sat down together looking out through their bay window and across the Irish Sea. John had continued to work for the Isle of Man Ferry company and now had 25 years' service despite still being reasonably young in seafaring terms. He was now one of the most experienced officers on the company and in the same way he had taken in every scrap of information given to him, he now mentored younger recruits sharing his experience and knowledge of the seas around the Isle of Man. He was often asked why he had not decided to see the world and whilst he did understand why people asked, he knew that each day gave him a different challenge with the weather and busy seas around the island ensuring there was rarely a dull moment. He also had the benefit of that daily challenge yet being home more nights than he was away, as well as his running it was not unusual for John to walk the three miles down to the sea terminal in Douglas prior to his shift, something he described as one of the best commutes in the world.

Despite always being a proud Lancastrian, his move to the Island over ten years ago had helped him advance within the company and the standard of living on the Island and the advantageous tax rates paid dividend too. His added benefit was when he did want to visit "home" that he could simply put his car on the ferry to Heysham or Liverpool at no charge and a short drive later he could be with his parents, the previous month he had even taken his mountain bike and cycled from

Heysham down the canal network from Lancaster passing through Garstang then Preston before arriving in Leyland a little more than 2 hours after the ferry had docked. But over the next few months these opportunities would become less likely, he looked over at Trudy and smiled and she grinned back at him, and he had to admit pregnancy really suited her. She was one of the reasons he had relocated, a proud resident of Laxey on the Island and reluctant to move away she had been working on the ferry as an apprentice engineer when they met and despite warnings from colleagues about working together the reality was they didn't see much of each other even when on shift at the same time given the difference in their roles. Trudy was now in a shore-based role and together they were planning significant maternity and paternity leave when the baby was born. There were now only a few weeks left, and their families were excited with Trudy's Mum visiting most days making the short journey down the coast from Laxey. Today they were attending their first Ante Natal class together at Nobles hospital just down in Douglas from where they lived. Although a relatively small hospital it served the whole island, and the facilities and reputation were excellent.

Trudy was almost ten years younger than John and although he had become well known on the Island given his position with the company Trudy had the benefit of being born and bred and it was unusual for them to go out and not recognise someone she knew, it was also fair to say she was the more outgoing of the two of them as well and she would naturally make friends wherever she went with her big smile and personality that immediately lit up a room. They had always known they wanted a baby but hadn't specifically planned for a date, John with his dry humour had suggested it was perfectly timed before the ferries got busy with the extra tourists and events that took place throughout the summer season. Pregnancy hadn't all ben plain sailing, Trudy had struggled with sickness early on and also didn't feel that John had done enough to be there at some of the key moments but she acknowledged that he had a responsible job and whilst the shifts were long they both benefitted from the days he had off shift, moving to a shore based role early in pregnancy also hadn't been ideal for Trudy and she felt the work she had been doing was less meaningful.

But today they were both excited to be going to the class together, Trudy was really pleased that John would at last get to meet her new friend Aimee and possibly her partner too. Apart from three years studying off the island at the University of Leeds where she had met friends from all over the UK, most of her life had been spent on the Isle of Man, although she had made great friends in her Uni days living on the Island hadn't made it easy to keep in touch so most of her friend were people she had grown up with on the island. This had made meeting Aimee extra special, they had met on Trudy's first appointment at the hospital when they had been in the waiting room together and immediately bonded as they started to talk and although in some ways their respective backgrounds and upbringings on different continents gave them little in common for some reason they just hit it off. Aimee had the ability to light up a room just like Trudy and talked and talked yet somehow left you knowing little about her life on the Island. Despite their different backgrounds they both found themselves enjoying pregnancy in their 40's, something else that had set them apart from others in the waiting room that day. They had met the day after their first appointment at a coffee shop down in Douglas just behind the promenade and had continued to meet at least once per week since. Aimee was enjoying pregnancy but missed her family who she hadn't seen for several years given the distance and work and she had started describing Trudy as her "sister".

John drove them down in to town using his parking space at the sea terminal where he was able to park even when off duty, from here it was a short walk to the coffee shop where Trudy and Aimee had been meeting, it had taken some persuasion to get Trudy in to the car as she was a big fan of the green benefits of using the excellent local public transport but with only a few weeks to go John had been insistent on driving particularly as there was a storm closing in.
John had questioned Trudy about Aimee and her partner, naturally shy he found it easier to know about

people before he met them but Trudy had told him in all honesty she knew very little about Aimee's partner other than he had a responsible job that sometimes took him "off Island". John had joked that he himself could make that claim and shrugged his shoulders but either way he knew that Trudy had enjoyed meeting Aimee and the least he could do was make the effort. After meeting at the coffee shop, they were going to head up to the hospital together where there was a class for both "mums and dads" together and both Trudy and Aimee had thought it a good idea for the prospective "dads" to meet first.

It was midweek and off season so the coffee shop was quiet when they entered, John scanned everyone seated knowing it would be easy to spot Aimee, as she herself joked with Trudy there weren't too many pregnant Africans on the island. As he held the door for Trudy he soon spotted Aimee with a beaming smile sat facing him to the rear of the café, Aimee must have recognised Trudy as well because he saw her nudge her partner and he turned and started to get up out of his seat as they closed the door behind them. As John walked towards them Aimee's partner was stood fully facing him and removed his glasses and John realised he was looking straight at his old friend Chris.

Chapter 21   March 2022 Isle of Man

Three days later John was on the bridge of the Isle of Man Ferry company flagship Ben My Chree as it made the routine crossing from Heysham to Douglas. He had brought the vessel out of the harbour himself at Heysham as there was a strong crosswind and then they initially headed southwest before turning and setting a mainly westerly path back towards the island. The ship was lightly loaded with passengers and the crossing was routine and although there was a slight swell on the Irish Sea today it was nothing either the ferry itself or the crew couldn't handle. Over the years he had made his reputation as someone who concentrated, sure of his own ability and sometimes quite serious but today his mind wandered a little as the ferry settled into its rhythm. He had been on duty since 7.30am that morning and they would land back in Douglas around 5.45pm meaning he would be on his way home around an hour later once he had handed over to the evening crossing master. He was still incredibly excited to know that in a few weeks' time he would be a father but seeing Chris out of the blue after over 20 years had totally thrown him. The five of them had been so close not just at school but for several years later and it had been a shock when not only had Dave disappeared in the Shetlands but Chris had also disappeared without trace. With Pete's career taking off and Colin taking a few risks too many of the friendships had simply fallen apart, whilst no one had fallen out with each other their togetherness just evaporated. They had all known that Chris was highly regarded in security circles and had mixed with the rich and famous but with the lack of word about his whereabouts they had presumed he was dead, his family couldn't reveal anything and the group knew that with the bond they had he would have contacted them if he was still alive wouldn't he?

They had agreed to meet that evening around 8pm as John wasn't on duty the following day and the company had a zero-tolerance position on employees of any rank having alcohol in their system. John loved being on duty at this time of year as the nights started to lighten and there was s sniff of summer in the air. As they approached Douglas Bay, he could see the promenade clearly and picked out the terminus tavern at the opposite end of the bay to the sea terminal where he had arranged to meet Chris that evening. The weather in Douglas was calm with visibility good so The Ben (as it was known to islanders) came in serenely and turned and backed on to the linkspan where it would soon unload both the freight and passenger traffic. As simple a manoeuvre as the team on duty made this look, in reality the Ben was about as big a ship as it was possible to get into the small harbour so it was paramount that everyone was alert. Once he received word that the ship was secure, he gave the order for disembarkation before starting the handover process then eventually heading home to Trudy who he would see briefly before meeting Chris. She had been almost as shocked as John to know that she had met a friend in Aimee who was in a relationship with one of John's childhood friends and at first was mega excited to make the connection and hoped that this could be the start of a special friendship between the two couples. It had been the first time she too had met Chris and whilst she had enjoyed meeting him she had found him hard to warm too, it wasn't anything he said, in fact it was probably what he didn't say that made him appear as he was in his own world.

She had also noted that John hadn't said too much about the meeting, it had clearly impacted him, but he had clammed up somewhat which she put down to the shock of seeing such a close friend after all the time that had passed. That evening she welcomed John at the door with a kiss and a cuddle and warmed up some food whilst he showered. He had been apologetic after arranging the meeting, but Trudy had told him not to be silly, it was amazing and such a coincidence that they simply had to meet again as there was so much to catch up on. After eating and changing Trudy admired him as he came downstairs, whether in his uniform or in the jeans and rugby shirt as he was now, she found it hard to resist him. He refused the lift down to the tavern saying it was only a 15-minute walk and he kissed her on the forehead, told her to call if he needed her and set off down the coast path to meet his old friend.

The terminus tavern was just a short walk along the coastal path and after dropping down on to the promenade he looked out to sea where he could just see the lights of "the ben" as it headed out to sea on its evening crossing to Heysham and in front of him the lights of Douglas twinkled. The terminus tavern was such named as it sat at the terminus of the electric tram railway that snaked its way up the island and the horse drawn trams that ran along the promenade in the summer season, both railways were used predominantly by tourists and didn't operate at this time of the evening so John walked along the tracks the last few hundred yards before crossing and entering through the front door to the pub. It was a traditional pub with a dining area that served food most days and a snug bar for those who just wanted to talk, drink and while the night away, they served locally brewed O'kells beer and John ordered a pint and sat in the window to keep an eye outside for Chris. Trade was light on a midweek evening, the food service had finished and there was a mix of customers some of whom were just arriving for the evening and a few who looked like they should have left for home already.

John saw someone walking along the promenade and he guessed with the stature, the way he was holding himself and the pace he was walking at that it must be Chris, he smiled to himself as he thought back to Chris joining the military and the times they had met up when he was on leave and before he knew it the door opened and Chris entered turning immediately to him as if he had known exactly where he was sat. He hadn't changed significantly since their school days, he was always lean, good looking and a confident air about him and always a feeling that there was a lot going on in his brain despite the calm exterior. John leapt up and gave him a man hug and shook his hand before buying him a pint and as he stood at the bar, he realised he felt quite emotional and his hands were shaking.

At first they made small talk, mainly about their respective partners and how pregnancy was going and the things they were going to do, prospective baby names and their hopes and dreams for their children, however both knew they were skirting round the edges and someone would have to dive in and fill over 20 years of gaps in the case of Chris but for now John was happy to let the conversation flow a little and not appear too eager. One thing that immediately hit John was how Chris answered questions, it wasn't that he didn't answer the questions it was that the answers were sometimes vague and incomplete. He strained his memory to remember Chris in his teens and thought to himself "yes, he has always been a bit like that". John asked some polite questions about where Chris lived on the island and the type of work he was involved in but the responses were "oh up in the north of the island" and "still doing private security work", whilst John understood there would be trust to re-build between them he didn't really understand why Chris would be secretive.

John talked about his career working on the Irish sea, how he and Trudy had met and their plans for the future, Chris listened intently and asked questions at all the right times but it didn't escape John that Chris was "wired", the slightest movement in the bar, if the door opened or a car pulled up outside he was immediately alert and his attention shifted.

John decided to walk back along the coastal path and up to his home, they had stayed for around 2 hours neither drinking too much but they had the impression that the landlord was keen to close with only a handful of customers left in the pub. As he walked back along the path he felt a strange type of excitement building up inside, he had found it hard to make friends on the island with his work and naturally shy disposition so to have an old friend "on tap" as they both went through the start of fatherhood in their 40's really excited him.

They had literally left the pub in different directions with Chris heading towards the centre of Douglas saying he was being picked up and he again strode purposefully all the way to the war memorial near the sea terminal where he got in the passenger side of a car which pulled away almost immediately.

Trudy was still awake when he got home, she had actually been a little nervous for John on how the meeting may go so was pleased that he had enjoyed himself, he explained that they would definitely be meeting again but one thing was puzzling him, as he had left Chris had embraced him and whispered in his ear "next time we meet remind me to tell you about Guernsey" and as Trudy gently drifted to sleep John lay there unable to drift off playing back in his mind his trip to Guernsey 20+ years ago on the Manx Maid.

Chapter 22   March 2022 Windermere

Adnan, Hussain, Tanweer and Shazad sat in a coffee shop between Bowness and Windermere after being dropped off way too early for their train to Oxenholme from where they would head home. This part of the Lake District was less scenic and more retail orientated, a far cry from some of the places they had been over the last week. The coffee shop was busy and most people didn't give them a second glance as they sipped on their coffee trying to make it last until the train was due. Over the last few days, it was very clear that Hussain had become the natural leader and the rest of them treated him as such hanging on his words. As they walked up to the station to catch the train towards their various destinations Adnan considered the last words of Hussain as they had left the coffee shop, and he had said "guys lets find our mission".

The train trundled to Kendal then climbed up to the mainline at Oxenholme, from here it would head on to Manchester airport but they were all due to disembark at Lancaster from where Adnan would travel to the Isle of Man to spend the rest of the school holiday with his family, Tanweer and Shazad were heading back to Leeds whilst Hussain said he had business to attend to in London. As the train crossed the River Lune into Lancaster Adnan had a strange mix of sadness to be saying goodbye to his friends but excitement for the future even though he didn't yet know what that held.

At Lancaster they said their goodbyes and Adnan crossed the footbridge to catch the local branch line train down to Heysham for the ferry to the Isle of Man. It had been a tight connection, and he had worried he may miss the train which literally ran just once per day to connect with the daytime ferry service but he needn't have worried as the train literally pulled in to the station as he reached the platform. Adnan took his seat placing his backpack on the overhead racks and put in his earphones to drown out the PA messages that no-one listened to. As he sat back he looked over to the opposite platform where he had originally arrived and saw Hussain stood waiting for his train to London, he could see he was involved in an animated conversation with someone, as the person turned Adnan saw it was the same person he had seen Hussain with at the outward bound centre on the first night and he couldn't help feeling that there were things that Hussain wasn't telling him.

Heysham port is situated 8 miles to the west of Lancaster and the train would take around 20 minutes stopping twice on the way, the train was not busy, and the majority of passengers got off at Morecambe with just a handful continuing down to the port for the ferry connection. Before the advent of car ferries Heysham port would have been a busy station with direct services across the north and even to London but the current station was a sad sight, a single platform with a bus type shelter and no facilities although it had the benefit of being just a minute's walk to the ferry terminal. Formalities at the port were relatively simple, although you were asked to carry ID this was classed as a domestic service so there was no immigration to complete and there was a cursory inspection of luggage with there being little logic to those picked out for a search and those left to pass through undisturbed. Within minutes he was sat in the waiting area and as the ferry hadn't yet arrived on its inbound service, he knew there would be a while to wait.

As well as the port the other significant development at Heysham was the power station which had been constructed in the early 1970's and Adnan grimaced at its ugliness as he looked through the waiting room window thinking what a far cry it was from the beautiful surroundings of the Lake District that he had experienced over the last few days.

The site is divided into two separately-managed nuclear power stations, Heysham 1 and Heysham 2, both with two advanced gas cooled reactors and it had been in the news recently as the government had completed a major re-build of the facilities rather than deactivate as had been planned and Heysham was also one of eight sites it considered suitable for future nuclear power stations. Whilst an eyesore and not popular with either locals or tourists it was without doubt a major boost for the economy and the planned reopening after refurbishment would be a major part of the current government's energy manifesto.

The Ben My Chree arrived in port and disembarked its passengers and mainly empty freight units that had come over from the island and within 15 minutes the foot passengers were boarding and the ferry left bang on time on its daily 2.15pm sailing. It slowly moved out of the harbour initially heading southwest before turning and heading north west from where it plotted pretty much a straight line across to the island where they would arrive some 3 ½ hours later. The weather was calm, so Adnan decided to spend time on deck looking north to the hills of the Lake District that he had just left behind before eventually having his first sight of the island out to the west. He was able to sit deep in his own thoughts without being disturbed and those thoughts turned to his home on the island and his parents. He had a difficult relationship with his father who he had never bonded with, there was nothing particularly he could put his finger on that had caused that difficult relationship but there just seemed to be a deep resentment into Adnans existence. On the other hand Adnan was closer to his mother, she led a reclusive lifestyle and to Adnans knowledge had never left the island during the last ten years. This wasn't particularly rare amongst islanders, but it was rare that she was also never seen outside the gates of the family home. Adnan could remember the few journeys he had made with his mother as a child and could not remember his mother speaking to anyone other than him and his father and although British Caucasian by birth, she had always worn a hijab or veil when in public places. His mother had never spoken about her own childhood or family, and it was almost like the life she had before Adnan had been erased from her memory. Only once had he seen this façade slip when he had heard his mother describe their home on the Isle of Man as a prison but when he had asked why she had never left she had stared into the distance and not answered.

The majority of passengers on the ferry were either returning home after visiting friends and family on the mainland or were tourists heading to attend the various festivals on the island. As the ferry got closer to the island more people came on to deck with passengers either glad to see their home or the tourists excited to see the island for the first time. There was a small cruise ship in the bay and Adnan could see the small boats returning the passengers after they had spent a day ashore on the island and a long blow on the horn from the Ben My Chree warned them of its imminent arrival in to the small harbour of Douglas. The ferry swung round 180 degrees stern first on to the linkspan and the first announcements were made for passenger disembarkation arrangements, as Adnan looked down on to Victoria Pier he knew neither his mother or father would be there to greet him but he immediately spotted the tall figure of Chris one of the families employees and he raised a hand in greeting, Chris however seemed to be staring up at the bridge before he turned and scoured the decks before focussing on Adnan and waving at him. After disembarking Adnan picked out Chris in the waiting area, he respected Chris more than his own father as he had spent hours kicking a ball with him as a little child or telling stories about his military days so it was with genuine warmth when he hugged him as the two men met in the waiting area. Chris had travelled down to the port in the Landrover Discovery and before he knew it he was heading out of town and to the north of the island to Jurby where the family home was, the island wasn't somewhere Adnan thought he would spend the rest of his life and nor could he say he missed it when he wasn't there but it was home and he was glad to be back for a short stay. It was a 30-minute journey up to Jurby and the traffic reduced as they left Douglas and Chris relaxed and started to fill Adnan in on the news from home. But Adnan was drifting away and all he could hear over and again in his mind was "lets find our mission".

The next morning he had breakfast with his parents, his mother looked well but like anyone not exposed to natural light regularly her face lacked colour, was wrinkled and despite her natural beauty she was starting to look older than her age. His father was unusually welcoming but like his mother he also seemed

to have aged recently and wore the expression of a man with the worries of the world on his shoulders.
The house was within a large compound close to an old airfield always busy with car and motorcycle enthusiasts, nothing about the property attracted interest, not its size, architecture or the security installations that protected it, it was indeed unremarkable. This was in in its own right remarkable as contained within its boundaries was potentially one of the most remarkable stories of recent history.

He had known most of the family story since his 12th birthday when his parents had deemed him old enough to understand, they had also made it clear that the next chapter of the family story wouldn't start until on or around his 21st birthday so he had always known this day would come, he had kept the family secret as he had promised but on that March morning back at the family home, as he learned about his parents plans for the future and the role they wanted him to play he could think only of his loyalty to his new friends Hussain, Shazad and Tanweer.

Chapter 23   March 2022 HMP Haverigg Cumbria

Around 65 miles to the east of the Isle of Man back on the mainland, Haverigg Prison sits on an old RAF airfield training centre and was opened in the 1960's with some of the Lake Districts hills as a backdrop. While some of the prison's workshops and offices were housed in buildings from that era, most of the prison had been extensively modernised over the years.

Haverigg Prison accepted relatively low risk prisoners or category D status who are able to participate in full-time employment. All prisoners take part in full-time employment or training with workshops, including manufacturing and horticulture. There is also a mental health department offering support for anxiety, depression and also more severe conditions. There is a visitors' reception centre outside the prison and a visitors' hall within the Prison which has a tea bar which provides hot and cold food and drinks and even a small children's play area both staffed by local volunteers. Prisoner 245668/1 had been in Haverigg for almost two years and was hoping for parole within the next 6 months, prior to Haverigg he had spent almost 14 years in various prisons across the north, but he had been happier here where he had certain freedoms and interactions with the outside world. As well as achieving significant levels of fitness he had studied hard and was now a qualified project manager and surveyor brought out on various visits and audits by officials to show what could be achieved in a well-run prison.

Like every other night in Haverigg he lay on his bed and considered the circumstances that had seen him end up in the prison system, initially arrested in 1998 as part of a murder investigation it was only when he was re-arrested a year later and interviewed under caution that his DNA had been taken, that DNA in turn had immediately yielded results on the Police database not for murder, but linked to the proceeds of the violent robbery of a Preston town centre bank in 1988.
Given the seriousness of the crime he had appeared before magistrates and been remanded in custody with no chance of bail, despite weeks of questioning he had refused to admit his involvement or indeed the involvement of any other person. A crown court date had eventually been set and after a three week trial he was found guilty on a unanimous verdict and the judge had jailed him for 25 years given the violent nature of the robbery, the impact it had on the victims and the fact that he refused to speak throughout the trial. He had not admitted anything nor incriminated anyone else and this had counted against him in his previous parole requests.

During his years in prison and particularly his time in Haverigg he had not had many visitors, he had been disowned by his family and most of the business associates he had known around the North West had disowned him as soon as he had been arrested. His lawyer had visited annually and advised him but this advice had generally been ignored in what his lawyer described as incredibly misplaced loyalties. But he had remained knowledgeable and sharp, as well as his studies he had read every day and also stayed abreast of news from the UK and around the world. Unusually for a prisoner he was popular with both staff and fellow inmates, he was someone that others could speak to and he generally helped prisoners who arrived at Haverigg for the first time, to all intents and purposes he did not fit with the typical profile of a long term prisoner in the penal system and he did not intend to stay in the system much longer.

During his time in prison the government had flip flopped between the two main parties and the party in power when he had originally been jailed were now in power again. During their first ten months back in power they had been surrounded by scandal and a leadership challenge had been sparked, the first round of voting had not gone well for the current prime minister and the smart money was on the Home Secretary to get the top job. Currently the three other candidates were holding hustings around the country in their bids to win the appropriate support and the media circus followed them and bookmakers laid odds on the next holder of the top job. He had been able to watch a live broadcast of the candidates up against each other in the live TV debate and he had smiled to himself as he recognised the candidates. What irony it was he had thought to himself that as a prisoner he didn't have the power to vote, but he did have the power to end the campaign of a front running prime ministerial candidate, the man who would be the first gay prime minister of the UK, his old friend from Leyland Pete Davison.

As he turned over hoping to find sleep he considered how life had gone and what the future held, he was sure that the next 25 years would be better than the last 25 years and it was time to start leaning on people.

The following morning Colin woke early and when his cell was opened he smiled broadly at the duty officer before being accompanied to his breakfast duties where he helped daily in the preparation of food. Later in the morning he used his allocated gym time to literally pound the treadmill covering almost 9 miles before showering and being ready for his lawyers visit early in the afternoon. They had been working on his next parole application but today Colin intended to drop a hand grenade in to the application, as his lawyer was about to leave and without the knowledge of prison staff Colin discretely passed a note to his lawyer, when his lawyer reached his car in the visitors car park and read it, he went white with shock.

Chapter 24   April 2022 Douglas Isle of Man

Aimee and Trudy met at their normal coffee shop but this time without their partners, Aimee had been unusually early and had smiled to herself that they still met in the coffee shop even though both of them had now cut caffeine out of their diets during her pregnancy. Despite her time on the island Aimee had never really got her head around the British obsession with clocks and the importance of time. In the remote village where she was raised life revolved around events and needs, not around false deadlines made against a ticking clock. Chris and Aimee's different backgrounds and upbringings led to lots of laughs in their relationship, often inappropriate in the politically correct landscape they lived in. Time wasn't one of them though, with his military background Chris was always punctual and when Aimee was late or paid no attention to time he would condescendingly describe her as being on "Africa time". Today though she was early as Chris had been coming in to Douglas to drop the families son Adnan back at the sea terminal as he travelled back to the mainland for his final term at school, she hadn't seen him for some time but had noticed a massive change that Chris hadn't picked up.

He just seemed to look happier, was more confident, friendlier and moved with purpose, something had changed within him she had explained to Chris. In the past he had treated her almost like he would a servant but now he was respectful and genuinely interested in her wellbeing and as he exited the land rover at the sea terminal he had kissed Aimee on both cheeks.

Aimee had also got out of the land rover at the sea terminal despite Chris's protestations, she wanted the fresh air and some exercise and with a withering look had told Chris "I'm pregnant not sick". She had immediately regretted walking despite her dismissing Chris, the wind had made it a difficult walk and then a squally shower had come in from nowhere and she had been glad to be early for Trudy and have the time to dry out and straighten herself. Although they had spoken on the phone it was the first time they had met face to face and Trudy was quite emotional when she saw Aimee's beaming face. They went through the normal small talk and laughed at Aimee's description of the weather on the island and the impact it had had on her natural hair, but Trudy was keen to know how Chris had been since he had met face to face alone with John and it wasn't long before she was interrogating Aimee. But Aimee didn't or couldn't give much away saying that even she after all these years sometimes found him hard to read.

She said he had been happy, even excited before the meeting and had certainly enjoyed the evening but since the meeting hadn't mentioned John much, it was as if he wanted to say something but couldn't.

Trudy laughed and said John's behaviour had been much the same, it was like Chris had opened up a chapter of John's life that he had buried away and only just started to read again and she thought he maybe needed some time to deal with things, after all as happy a coincidence as it had been it must also have been a shock to both of them.

They both chatted excitedly about the forthcoming babies moving away from the topic of Chris and John and Aimee cried as she described Trudy as the sister from a different mister before they both ended up in fits of giggles attracting the stares of other customers in the coffee shop. Not long after they grabbed their coats getting ready to leave with Aimee vehemently refusing the offer of a lift home with Trudy which would have taken her well out of her way, she had instead arranged for Chris to come back to collect her as there were things they wanted to shop for together ready for the new arrival they were due to welcome. They embraced and were about to part when Trudy said "oh John just text – he said he thought he saw you and Chris dropping someone off at the sea terminal as he was starting his shift and it looked like he was catching the ferry, he just wondered who it was as John is in command of the ferry over to Heysham this morning? ". For the first time in their friendship Aimee had struggled for an answer before saying John must have been mistaken, something that knowing John, Trudy found hard to believe.

The Ben My Chree had left bang on time easing off its berth with a busy load of passengers and freight exiting the harbour and gradually picking up speed and heading east for Heysham, some island residents said you could almost set your clock by its departures and although occasionally there were weather delays cancellations ran at less than 1%. This morning John was in command although he had decided to let his first officer take charge on the outward crossing as he wanted to spend some time both with the engineering staff and those working in passenger areas and he would only come back up to the bridge of the ferry for the final approach in to Heysham. Whilst most passengers would only interact with a handful of the crew the reality was on board there were around 50 crew members for each crossing. Whilst John rightly spent most time on the bridge he was always keen to understand the challenges of the rest of the crew being a leader, not just the ships commanding officer.

Today he spent some time with the chief engineer and they discussed forthcoming maintenance that was required on its annual visit to the dry dockyard on the river Mersey across from Liverpool, this needed to be timed like clockwork with relief vessels having to cover the crossings so ensuring all the right parts and skills in place was paramount. He then passed through to the passenger areas speaking to several passengers on the way and stopping to chat to a couple of islanders that he recognised. There were not a huge amount of facilities on board, just two café/bars and a small number of cabins for the 3 1/2 hour crossing, there was also a lack of reliable Wi-Fi which was a frequent complaint so he was keen to understand the current opinions of passengers which had hopefully been considered in the design of the replacement vessel. As he passed in to the main passenger lounge, he recognised the young man who he thought he had seen getting out of Chris's vehicle, he tried to make eye contact but he had a passive expression on his face and was staring in to the distance, John couldn't help thinking that other than seeing him earlier that day he had seen the face before somewhere, something that was to trouble him for the rest of the voyage. He knew Chris didn't have any children yet although he was old enough to be this young man's father, he looked like he had some middle eastern heritage and his skin was a lovely light brown colour and as he looked over again at him from the opposite side of the ship he noticed that he was attracting the attention of several girls at the bar who were pointing at him and giggling.

Adnan had spent the majority of the voyage in the same seat, on previous crossings he would probably have used his general parental allowance to buy a seat in the business lounge but spending time with Hussain, Tanweer and Shazad had made him re-evaluate the value of money and instead he kept the money safely in his pocket.

He had always known his parents would have a discussion with him at some point and there would always have to be a resolution to the family secret, moreover he always knew that he would probably be part of the resolution and he had listened carefully to his father and nodded in all the right places also smiling at his mother whilst they discussed their plans for the next few months. His parents had appeared pleased that he had agreed with everything and that he had said he would play his role exactly as they wished, he had agreed to visit the island home again during the short school break in May when final plans would be laid down. But inside he felt disgusted by their greed, by their self importance and need for revenge, already a plan was starting to form in his head and he smiled to himself when he thought that with a few simple changes their plan could be just what he was looking for and once again that warm excited feeling welled up deep inside his stomach.

John was back up on the bridge with his first officer as the Ben My Chree entered Morecambe bay where it turned and made a line directly for Heysham, the entrance to the harbour was not easy, even on a relatively calm day like today but as he had a qualified certificate for Heysham he could take command of the vessel without the local pilot having to come aboard.

The first officer ceded control back to "the boss" and John focussed himself on the last few minutes of the crossing, as he looked ahead he saw an image in front of him and he realised where he had seen the boy's face before.

Chapter 25   April 2022 Otley West Yorkshire

Otley is a traditional Yorkshire market town with a population of around 14,000 situated on the River Wharfe around 10 miles west of Leeds. It is the sort of place that people settle for as it gives them access to work in the nearby cities of Leeds and Bradford yet also has some of the most beautiful Dales countryside on its doorstep for walkers, runners and cyclists. Famed for the number of pubs and its various festivals it is the sort of town that you can feel part of the community yet hidden away at the same time. As well as a weekly cattle market there are three vibrant food and produce markets a week and tourists visit to see where scenes from the long running British soap opera Emmerdale are filmed.

Half a mile East of the town on the road towards Pool there is a nondescript road, East Busk Lane, that starts off with houses and slowly becomes greener before turning into a traditional farm track. It is known to regular walkers, runners and the people that live on the road but virtually unknown to most people, that was why a safe house had been situated there almost since the end of the second world war that was shared between both British Intelligence and American counterparts. Colin was walking back to the house from the town of Otley and mused to himself that it was the most obvious "safe house" possible with fencing around it and a blacked out range rover on the driveway and communications equipment on the roof. Maybe, he thought, it was so obvious that people would think it wasn't obvious? He had settled in-to a good routine since arriving and each morning, although tagged, he went for a 10 mile run firstly along the busy roads then through several of the local villages following the River Washburn and then back over the hill and into Otley. At school he had hated running but during his time inside he had learned the benefits it was bringing to both his mental and physical wellbeing, his morning run was now taking him around 75 minutes and each day he tried to be slightly quicker than the last. In the afternoon he walked into town generally to get supplies or complete any other errands needed for the house, the rest of the day he stayed inside and was instructed not to use the small garden area.

His release from Haverigg had happened really quickly, several weeks after he had given his instructions the lawyer had returned to say his release was imminent and sure enough a week later he had been called to the governor's office, his few belongings were returned to him and he was made ready for departure. The governor had looked at him quizzically, almost with pity before explaining to him that his release had been approved by the outgoing former Home Secretary and Prime Minister in waiting Pete Davidson. There were caveats though and on departure day rather than being allowed to leave via the main gates of Haverigg he had been bundled in to a darkened SUV and driven for 2.5 hours down to Otley where he now was. Since arriving he had been designated a handler who had given him basic instructions and he was left in no uncertain terms as to what the end result would be if he broke the restrictions that were put in place. At first this hadn't bothered him too much as there was no family, girlfriend or close friends for him to visit, he had no wish to start drinking again and his time inside had left him shy when it came to conversation so the evenings were spent watching current affairs and news.

After almost three weeks at the house his handler informed him that he would be meeting a colleague but that the meeting would take place away from the "house". so he found himself sat on a bench in the park by the river Wharfe at 11am each morning waiting for the contact to arrive. Today was the 5th day he had sat and waited without anyone turning up and he was beginning to feel like he was being tested. The park was busy most days with pre school children on the playground and others just walking their dogs. After the third day he started to recognise the same people and thought it was strange how they seemed to arrive at the same time, but then again they might be thinking the same about me, he thought. By the 5th day he had worked out that if he entered the park from the entrance closer to town he could bring in an artisan coffee that he would sip at whilst he waited, these simple luxuries he had missed for so many years. Finally on the 8th day as he sat on the bench he was joined by another man, he sat there saying nothing, much older than Colin had expected but he had appeared almost out of thin air and was as nondescript as nondescript could be. On that day just as about Colin had been about to speak the man had stood up and walked off and it wasn't until day 11 at exactly the same time that he appeared again and this time he had spoken. Indeed he spoke for the next three days, never allowing Colin to ask a question and raising his hand in protest if he tried to.

On the first day Colin had listened with disbelief as the man had described his childhood, his friends, his early career and incarceration in the British prison system. On the second day he went into detail about his friends John, Pete, Dave and Chris, in fact it was incredible detail about what they had been doing over the last few years, their families, spouses, new friends and careers, very little was left untouched. The information was so detailed that Colin started to feel physically sick, where was this going and most importantly why was he being told and what would be expected of him? The next day he pretty much found out, the previous day he had been told to be in a different location this time much closer to the weir in the River Wharfe that took the water out to the Ouse and eventually the North Sea.

They again sat on the bench and Colin listened, at times having to strain to hear against the backdrop of the water behind them. The man explained what was expected of Colin, where he would be going, when and what he had to do, in fairness on paper it hadn't sounded too difficult but he knew this was probably not the case. Although he had been told not to ask questions he couldn't help asking "what's in it for me?", the man stood and began to walk back towards town before turning towards Colin, half smiling and mouthing "life" to him.

Ten days later, following instructions, he had ordered a taxi to take him the short 10 minute ride up to Leeds Bradford airport, the airport was busy with holiday flights mainly to Spain and its islands but tucked away at the back of the terminal were the check in desks for scheduled flights to Belfast, Dublin and the Isle of Man. One hour later he found himself sat at the back of the small propellor driven plane with around 25 other passengers on the short flight to the Isle of Man and less than an hour later he was exiting the terminal at Ronaldsway airport and looking for a taxi to take him in to the principal town on the island, Douglas.

Chapter 26   April 2022 North Yorkshire

Adnan had returned to his school lodgings after the Easter Break in the Lake District and Isle of Man and was already planning his next holiday period where he again hoped to meet with Tanweer, Hussain and Shazad. Most evenings he chatted on line with Hussain either via chat room or WhatsApp and Hussain would take a greater interest each night in Adnans background and plans for the future. Gradually the conversations became more intense and Hussain eventually commented that it was probably better they only shared their thoughts and hopes face to face. So a week after returning and on the first available Saturday Adnan found himself on the bus to Leeds, this week the bus was full of people either shopping or travelling to watch the Leeds United game that afternoon. Adnan zoned out from the excited chatter, inserted his headphones and listened to some of the podcasts sent to him by Hussain. The content was close to his heart with tales of being marginalised from society, the struggle that he and his "brothers" faced living in the UK and stories of those who had chosen Jihad to banish western ideals from their homelands. He looked around the bus and realised how much he despised the people around him, the society he once yearned to be part of just sickened him and he felt the need and pride to play his part in making things right.

After arriving in Leeds Adnan caught a bus out to Headingley where he met the others in the Costa Café on Otley Road, it was their first meeting since the Lake District and their welcome and greetings were genuine as they caught up and reminded each other of the things they had done together. Just over an hour later they were in a taxi to Beeston, the other side of the city, where they visited Hussains mosque meeting several of the elders in the community room to the rear. During the afternoon they discussed studies, the struggles and what the future looked like but all too soon Adnan was reversing his steps and heading for the bus station for the return journey to school. Hussain walked with him whilst the others headed off in the opposite direction, at first the chat was mundane but the closer they go to the bus station the more intense the chatter came. As Adnan was about to board the bus Hussain embraced him and whispered in his ear, Adnan almost stumbled with pride but shock when Hussain explained the elders wanted him to join Hussain on a trip to Africa to further his studies and they felt his background and special story made him a unique part of the team.

So in the May school holiday he found himself on a Kenya Airways flight from Amsterdam after taking the regular morning flight from Leeds Bradford Airport to make the connection. It was a long 9 hour flight from Amsterdam down to East Africa and the Kenyan capital Nairobi, he had been told to bring carry on luggage and one case and to dress very much as a tourist heading either on safari or the beaches on the east coast of Africa. The flight was uneventful and he had watched a movie and read about the country he was visiting, it was not where he had expected when he had been told he would be training with brothers ready to deliver their mission later in the year. It was Hussain who had explained that their normal routes were all compromised, previous bases in Somalia, Sudan and Pakistan had been infiltrated so they were going to be hosted by a small group in Mombasa, right in the middle of a town surrounded by European tourists.

In Nairobi Adnan had swapped terminals and then taken the short flight across to Mombasa where he had landed less than an hour later and within 15 minutes he was collecting his luggage and exiting the terminal from where he took a taxi to the address he had been given in the old town of Mombasa close to the tourist destination of Fort Jesus. The fort and indeed the town had changed hands on multiple occasions with colonial masters ranging from the Ottomans and Portuguese through to the British who had ruled through until Kenyan independence. The taxi weaved its way through the streets whose architecture was mainly Swahili but also influenced by its colonial past and more modern Islamic styles. The streets were busy and they passed the spice market and weaved their way between modern 4x4's and motorised rickshaws all sharing the tiny space. Despite the throngs of people, smell and dirty streets Adnan was excited, it was his first time in Africa and it had indeed turned out to be much like he had read in the guide on the flight down. The taxi turned into Berkeley Place, surely a hangover from British Rule, and shortly stopped outside a small guest house. He entered through the front door and was immediately met by a familiar face, it took Adnan only seconds to realise it was the guy that he had seen Hussain talking to by the lake in Cumbria when they had visited the Lake District, he offered Adnan only the briefest of welcomes before he was told to hand over his passport, wallet and anything else that might identify him. He was then shown to his spartan room and told not to leave it until someone came to collect him.

However Adnan wasn't going anywhere anyway, the day had caught up with him and he found sleep came easily and he slept right through to 5am the following morning when he was woken by the traditional call for prayers coming from the Shia mosque close to where he was staying. At first he struggled to remember where he was and felt like he was waking from a strange dream, but as he saw his luggage in the corner of the room and felt the heat even at this early hour he soon remembered. Within minutes of waking there was a knock at the door and as he opened it he found a mixture of fruits, bread and a green tea had been left for him as well as a handwritten note telling him to be downstairs by 6am.

He made sure he was ready on time and was dressed in standard tourist attire to blend in to the city, even at this early hour the traffic was busy as they stepped out as the city was very much a trading post and gateway to East Africa with container ships arriving with goods from all over the world. There was also tourist traffic about with some keen to miss the hot sun later in the day and others setting out on safari to the countries game reserves many hours drive away. His driver Arnold first took him to some of the city sights, and whilst they didn't leave the vehicle he was told the story of the city, the significance of Fort Jesus and various stories of how the Ottomans, Portugeuse and British had all left their mark here. They then headed out of the city through the huge elephant tusks that had been erected in the 1950's to celebrate the visit of Queen Elizabeth and the irony of this symbolism and his home country was not lost on Adnan. These days China seemed to be setting the Geopolitics of the region and the railway they witnessed snaking out of Mombasa to the capital in Nairobi was an example of their investment.

They headed to the beaches of Bamburi and amongst the rocks and under the cliffs adjacent to the Indian Ocean he met three comrades who were also going through a similar training programme, despite their shared beliefs and commitments they would all be working on separate missions which they were forbidden to talk about and nor were they able to establish each others names or origins.

Much had been written about training camps in the British press but generally the camps were in places such as Syria, Pakistan, The Sudan and Somalia. Adnan had never imagined he would be training right here on a tourist beach amongst his compatriots. Listening to the accents he could hear British and German predominantly mainly elderly and generally relaxing after a week exploring the inner country on safari. Many of the holidaymakers stayed on their hotel premises but when the moved to the beach locals were there waiting offering trips, cruises, massages and souvenirs. Also common were single European males looking to meet locals which put together made the beach an interesting place to people watch.

The morning was spent building up physical fitness with runs along the beach with muscles being tested in the soft sand, this continued for hours without water and Adnan had got to a point where he felt he couldn't carry on further when thankfully the session was brought to a close and they were taken to what looked like an abandoned hotel. The Ocean View had once been a four star hotel attracting both tourist trade as well as conventions, weddings and business meetings but a combination of poor management and Covid-19 had resulted in closure and the property was now boarded up with a very eery feel to it. Here they spent the afternoon learning martial arts and eating a basic lunch together before being taken back to their separate residences at the end of the day. This continued for 6 days until Adnan was told to pack his belongings as he would be returning to the UK, the location and period of training had been designed to create minimal risk and he would be back in the UK and at his school before family, teachers and fellow pupils asked any questions about his whereabouts. He checked in at Mombasa airport without anyone raising an eyebrow entering the prayer room in the domestic terminal before his flight was called to Nairobi and several hours later he was boarding the flight from Nairobi back to the UK via Amsterdam. Before he had left Kenyan soil a message was received back in the UK stating that Adnan was battle ready from both a mental and physical point of view, unbeknown to himself he had passed the test.

Chapter 27   May 2022 Douglas Isle of Man

Colin stepped out of the taxi and checked in to the Mereside hotel just off the main promenade in Douglas, it was typical of many of the establishments which had been built in the heyday of tourism. He was given a warm welcome and rundown of all the facilities and meal times and he explained as part of his cover story that he had a contract to work on the island and wasn't certain how long he would be here. His room overlooked the sea and had the basic facilities he needed for his stay, after all he had thought to himself it was still a novelty to him knowing that no-one would come and lock the door at 10pm and he could come and go as he pleased. After unpacking he headed out on the promenade for a run keen to work out a regular route to keep up his daily exercise whilst also giving him the opportunity to integrate into daily life and work out the local routines. It was a windy evening and despite his fitness he found it tough running into the headwind but then had the pleasure of the wind behind him on the way back. He picked up some leaflets and an island map from the hotel lobby and worked out how he would reach the settlement of Jurby the next day. He had been given an address in the north of the island to observe as well as providing details of the various routes someone could possibly take from the address down to the ferry terminal in Douglas. It had been a long time since he had been on the island when he had sat in the prospect pub meeting a business contact prior to spending time with his old mate John on the ferry back across to mainland UK. Colin had wondered whether John still worked on the ferries and whether their paths may cross, however he had been told that whilst his role was not totally covert he was not to form any relationships during his time on the island, he had also been told that as far as the UK government was concerned if he did get in to trouble they would deny any knowledge of him and the operation he was undertaking. He had also wondered why he had been chosen, he had no prior experience of such work and he was sure there must be people better placed than himself but he didn't dwell on it and instead continued to work on his business plan aimed at taking back control of his various businesses in Lancashire once this work was over.

The following morning he took a bus up to Ramsey, a small port town on the northeast of the island and took some time to familiarise himself with the town. It was the northern terminus of the quaint electric tramway that ran along the island with the heartbeat of the town nestled round the harbour side. After an hour, taking a morning coffee in the bustling café where he had listened in to various conversations , he caught another bus across to Jurby where he alighted, put on his small backpack and tried to look every bit the off season walker whilst keeping his eyes peeled in his search for the family home he had been told to find. He thought he was in the right place but not wanting to draw attention he kept walking and eventually ended up back at one of the islands main roads from where he caught a bus back to Douglas. As he reflected on the day Colin considered it to be successful, he had got a good feel for the geography of the island and was pretty certain he had found the family home he had been told to locate, his cover story had worked well too as he had left the hotel around 8.30am returning just after 5pm which for anyone who may be observing pretty much mirrored the standard working day around the island. He wasn't in the mood for small talk this evening so after a short run up and down the promenade he decided to visit a local grocery store and buy a sandwich and snacks to eat in his room along with a copy of the local newspaper. The local newspaper led with a story about the new ferry that had arrived on the island, the link to the UK mainland was the primary route for all goods on to the island so Colin guessed it would be a big deal to most people. It was rumoured that Prince Charles was to name the new ship, but the locals were outraged that this would likely happen on the UK mainland and not in the harbour at the new vessels home port. The next morning Colin stepped out at around the same time but this time sat and waited for the train to take him over to the west side of the island where he visited Port Erin and then caught a bus from there to the Port of Peel where he made himself familiar with the layout of the port and main street where most of the shops were situated interspersed with a number of cafes and takeaways. He arrived back in Douglas at roughly the same time as the previous day and retraced his steps to the hotel arriving at a similar time. As he considered his day, he realised he had seen most of the island, understood the infrastructure and without further instruction he wasn't certain what more he could do other than confirm the house he had seen was indeed the family home he had been told to locate. After changing out of his slightly damp clothes, after being caught in a shower earlier, he headed back out on to the promenade where he noticed the ferry arriving on its regular daytime service from Heysham. His plan had been to try and work out its routine but by the time he reached the sea terminal it seemed the majority of vehicles had already left the ship and there was a stream of taxi's who had collected foot passengers as well as some people choosing to walk down the promenade to their final destination. At the southern end of the promenade there is a statue to commemorate one of the islands best known island families the Bee Gees, as he passed he noticed a couple of young lads with distinctly Yorkshire accents, they were acting in a way that youngsters do when they are away from families on their own, excited and not a care in the world or so it seemed. One of them asked if Colin would take a photo of them with the statue which he did and the elder looking one said thanks it was their first holiday away without their families. At first Colin thought how funny it was that indeed he had been correct and they were on holiday before thinking to himself what a strange place for two young lads to visit for their first holiday away together. As he kept walking towards the ferry terminal, he heard a voice behind shout "come on Tanweer we need to find that bus to Ramsay".

As he walked back towards the hotel, he heard the phone he had been given vibrating in his pocket and he ducked in to a shelter on the promenade to get out of the wind and answer the call. He recognised the voice the other end even though there were no pleasantries, without asking him how he was and how the assignment was progressing the voice simply said "you will be there another 6 weeks and we expect a significant event will bring a close to your time on the island, you should work out the location of your old friend John and let it be known that you are working on the island".

Approximately 65 miles east of Colins location the staff at Heysham power station had been celebrating the news that their facility was being refurbished and its life extended, it was a huge employer in the area and many families depended on it for income as it provided employment for many subsidiary and local businesses too. The facilities manager, Gary Herbert, was responsible for making sure the property was well maintained, efficient and the correct environment was provided for those who worked there. It was his last year in the role as he had chosen to retire but it had been confirmed that morning that they were to receive a royal visitor during the first week of July, Prince Charles would travel with his consort Camila and visit the wind farms of Morecambe Bay, the power station and would also be naming a new ferry in the adjacent harbour. As part of the recognition of his 30+ years' service it had been confirmed Gary would meet the Prince and as he left work for the day he had a spring in his step as he rushed home excited to tell his wife, children and grandchildren, it really did feel like one of the proudest moments of his life.

Adnan had settled back into school life well in North Yorkshire after his short trip to East Africa and despite his excitement he had not shared anything about the journey to school friends and in fact had become more and more withdrawn. Being a private school the end of term was fast approaching, and he would travel back to the family home on the island on the 2nd July. His mother had sent him a text message the previous night saying she wanted him straight home as the plan was to be implemented soon after his arrival.

Chapter 28   July 2022 Isle of Man

Colin had been on the island for nearly two months and had settled into a routine where he left the small hotel each morning returning at the end of the day, as far as anyone observing him at the hotel would think he was out at work as he had stated he would be when he arrived. This had led to some long hours walking and diving in and out of coffee shops to avoid the frequent showers in this rather wet June, but he felt he had done everything asked of him. It had taken him less than half an hour to track down John once he had been given the instruction, he was indeed still working for the ferry company and from his social media updates he had deduced that he was settled on the island with a wife and very young baby. For obvious reasons through his time "inside" Colin didn't have a social media presence and had taken several days to build up a credible Facebook account before contacting John who had then taken several days to reply. Colin had known he would need a cover story and via several messages had explained to John that he was on the island in a role as consultant advising hospitality businesses. Eventually John had agreed to meet but due to the pressures of his shifts and new family he had asked Colin if they could meet by the ferry terminal initially and walk/talk as John walked home and up to his house at Onchan. As they walked John had brought Colin up to date with his life both at home and his career at sea but hadn't really enquired too much about Colin probably as he knew full well where Colin had been in recent years but there was also a coolness in John that had made Colin feel that he was meeting out of politeness rather than any great wish to see him. However, they had swapped numbers and John had mumbled pleasantries about seeing each other again and visiting and meeting his wife and new baby and that he would be in touch. What had really surprised Colin, however, was the fact that John hadn't mentioned their other friend Chris who he knew was on the island, surely if he had nothing to hide he would mention that a friend from their school days was living nearby?

After leaving Colin, John had hurried onwards up the remaining promenade to his home excited to see his wife and baby yet exhausted from his shift and the catch up from several nights of broken sleep. But at the back of his mind he was also thinking about the meeting with Colin, something hadn't added up in his reasoning for being on the island and it hardly sounded like the sort of work Colin would be involved in despite his period inside following the events of years ago. John couldn't pinpoint exactly why he hadn't mentioned Chris to Colin but the fact that three of them were now on this small island seemed too much of a coincidence, in a few short weeks the memories of his past had blended into his present and it didn't feel good.

Further up the island in Ramsay, Tanweer and Hussain had rented an Airbnb apartment close to the harbour side, it had taken them only a few days after their arrival to get familiar with the local geography and they had settled in to a routine of planning their mission only leaving the apartment for occasional recce's of the vessels in the harbour and to get additional supplies from the local Coop.

Over the previous week Hussain had been tracking the movements of a small general cargo ship, Silver Wind, less than 500 tonnes in weight that plied its trade between Ramsey on the island, Belfast in Northern Ireland and Glasson Dock on the UK mainland. Apart from the ferries that ran from Douglas this was the only other regular service from the island normally carrying building materials and agricultural fertilisers for use on the island. It was more than 50 years old and made slow progress of normally around 8 hours in whichever direction it went but was ultra reliable and served its main purpose of being able to fit into the harbours of the Isle of Man and Glasson Dock on the mainland. Crewed by only four people it would be the perfect vehicle for the mission and Hussein had been interrogating the company website to find its schedule and how this fitted with their plans. Hussein had also followed two of the crew as they had returned from the mainland on a Friday evening and sat close by as they entered the harbour side inn. The small crew were mainly elderly, all of them experienced but now happy to work on this regular service close to home and rarely away from the island for more than two nights at a time. The following day he had met the others and had told them that the vessel would indeed be perfect for their mission which was now confirmed as on and the group should start to plan how they would board, hide and take control of it.

Later that day Hussein met Adnan in Port Erin and confirmed that the mission was on, on the 5th July, Adnan had only been back on the island for one night but had sat with his parents as they had explained the plans and their expectations of Adnan. He had sat their silently looking shocked saying little but confirming in what he had hoped sounded genuinely reluctant that they expected this of him whilst inside feeling a warm and excited feeling that he would be able to be part of one of the biggest news stories of the millennium.

As Adnan was meeting Hussein in Port Erin Dada summoned Chris to his office in the family home and explained what the family were planning over the next few days. To say Chris was surprised was an understatement and it was all he could do to keep his cool despite his reputation for giving very little away. Normally he was able to assess each situation for his boss dispassionately, but this was going to have a major impact on the life Aimee and himself had built on the island and in particular recently with their new baby.

As Dada had spoken to Chris his voice had been slightly shaken suggesting he was nervous, however it was clear from the extent of what was being suggested that this had been in the planning for several years, this frustrated Chris even more that all this planning and associated security detail had been thought through without his input. His initial thought was he needed to speak to someone, but he didn't know who, he didn't want to unduly worry Aimee and he had deliberately kept few friends on the island. He was due to meet John the following evening, but he knew he was also dealing with being a new father and his stressful job as master on the new ferry. In the end Chris decided to speak to the commanding officer at his old military unit the Queens Lancashire Regiment who had served with him at the time and he felt he could trust with his life, what he didn't realise by doing so was that he was setting off a chain events that was to be life changing for all involved.

As he spoke to his wife John was so excited he could barely get his words out, it was like his mouth couldn't keep up with the speed his brain wanted to work at. The new island ferry was being officially named by Prince Charles in 72 hours and he had been chosen to take the ferry across to Heysham on its regular sailing and would meet the Prince as the ferry was named in between sailings along with a group of island VIP's who would travel across too. The Prince was in Heysham to launch a green energy initiative at the power station and would also visit the wind farms in Morecambe Bay before boarding the ferry and having lunch with the assembled dignitaries.

Chapter 29   Ramsey Isle of Man

The Silver Wind headed out of Ramsey on a perfectly clear day, the tide high enough for them to exit the harbour and pass into the North Sea. In the distance the skipper could make out the distant hills of the Lake District in England as well as the lowlands of Southwest Scotland and various commercial vessels passing between Scotland/Ireland and England. They would pass around the north of the Island hugging the coast passing close to the Point of Ayre at the northernmost tip of the island before plotting a course for Belfast which at their speed of around 8 knots would take them 8 hours to reach. The small cargo ship was high in the water with nothing in the hold, but they were due to have a short layover in the Northern Irish capital before returning just a few hours later to Ramsey and then on to Glasson Dock England. This was a busy channel with a mix of cruise ships, passenger and freight roll on/roll off ferries and the various bulk and container carriers delivering their goods around the British Isles or heading out across the Atlantic to the Americas. Belfast had changed mused the skipper since his early days visiting Northern Ireland, there had been a lot of construction in the last twenty years and the port area, whilst still busy, had changed beyond recognition becoming a tourist destination in its own right with people travelling from around the globe to learn the story of the Titanic built in the Harland and Woolf yard close to the city centre. They would dock close to the Titanic Museum, and he would rest whilst the crew worked to load the vessel and return them back in to the Irish Sea before sunset, todays load was fertiliser for the island and Kerosene which was going onwards to Glasson Dock. The irony of such an explosive cargo in this troubled city wasn't lost on him, but as he thought to himself things had moved on considerably in the last 20 years. The service they provided was the only regular service connecting Northern Ireland which was booked through a small office in Ramsey on the Isle of Man. In previous years the transport would have been heavily checked and regulated but since the trouble's checks had become more lax and less frequent. The broker in Ramsey had notified the skipper of a small consignment that would be loaded today and stay in the hold until their subsequent trip over to Glasson Dock the following day. The consignment had arrived and been loaded just before they left and was sat in the hold, The skipper frowned and wondered why such a small consignment was being shipped in this way but then shrugged and reasoned that it wasn't his job to question orders from the office in Ramsey.

After loading had completed, they headed back down the river Lagan and out to sea through Belfast Lough following the passenger ferry bound for its short crossing to Stranraer. Passing Carrickfergus on the Port side and the seaside town of Bangor on the starboard side he looked out across to Scotland and Stranraer, although a mere 25 miles away the weather had closed in, and Scotland was only just visible in the distance. The passenger ferry had already pulled away with its superior size as he set the autopilot southwest and back to their home port of Ramsey. Whilst the weather had closed in, he was still expecting an easy crossing with winds force 4-5 and a reasonable swell, whilst old this vessel would take them home safely and comfortably. Whilst still close to land he switched on his iPad and read the news from the isle of man via the digital publication IOM today. Over the last few weeks, the news had been dominated by the arrival of the new flagship passenger ferry which was due to make its maiden fee earning crossing to Heysham the following day. A huge investment for the island he smiled at all the "social media" captains who were commenting and already writing off this new investment for the island before its first commercial sailing.

The crossing to Ramsey was uneventful with the winds dropping even further and the skipper dropped anchor in Ramsey Bay whilst they waited for the tide to rise so they could enter the harbour. As dawn broke the silver Wind passed through the harbour and tied up, the skipper and the crew briefly headed home to refresh before they were back on shift just three hours later, in the meantime the shore crew got to work unloading the hold then loading the small number of items due to travel to Glasson Dock later that morning.

Ramsey was extremely quiet with many of the seafarers and in some cases their vessels heading down to Douglas to watch the departure of the new flagship ferry on its inaugural voyage to Heysham. The guys loading the silver wind worked backwards and forwards from the main road, at a point when they were unloading a trailer off the main road by the quayside three shadows emerged from a disused shed on the harbour wall leapt on to the silver wind and secreted themselves in the bow area of the ship. The final items were loaded, the hold closed before the skipper and his crew returned ready to lead the busy little cargo carrier back out into the Irish Sea. The skipper accelerated to the higher end of the little ships capacity and the engines worked hard as they headed South East towards Glasson Dock, he was determined to see the new flagship ferry on its journey to Heysham and at current reckoning they would cross each other's path in around 5 hours time as both vessels were on their final approach in Morecambe Bay to their final destinations.

Chapter 30   London

Pete was in the back of a reinforced ministerial Range Rover on the way out to RAF Northolt west of London. As he looked out of the darkened windows he could see the traffic being held at junctions allowing his convoy to pass unhindered with pedestrians trying to peer in to the vehicle to see who it was that was so important that they had an escort front, behind and at each side focussed on keeping them moving through the busy rush hour traffic. Since becoming Prime Minister life had been a whirlwind with global media reflecting on his career, partner and the fact he was the first British PM to come through the comprehensive school system. His private secretary was sat in the front seat busily studying the timetable for the day and making one final call to the royal entourage who they would meet later in the day. He sat back wrapping his arms behind the headrest closing his eyes and running the journey of his life through his mind to this point, he still couldn't quite believe, and inwardly suffered insecurities, about the position he had found himself in. After passing by Kensington, Earls Court and Hammersmith they branched over towards Northolt and as he looked south, he could see the regular passenger aircraft arriving in to Heathrow at incredibly short intervals.

They swept into RAF Northolt and straight to the waiting jet that would take them north firstly to

Cumbria. The red top media had seized on his frequent use of air transport but his focus had remained on social reform, reducing the deficit, education and improving transport connectivity for the wider public, one thing he had discovered, and struggled with, was the constant digging and negativity of the media and learning not to take too much notice of it but overall he had a good feeling as he walked up the steps and on to the waiting aircraft.

As soon as the door closed the engines roared into life and they were taxiing down the runway taking off in a Westerly direction heading out towards the border with Wales eventually before turning north and making a straight line for Cumbria. Somewhere down below the Prince of Wales and his consort were on the Royal Train also heading north and after an appointment at a new electric vehicle manufacturing facility near Crewe the Royal Train would continue to the Northwest where they would meet Pete and his entourage later in the day.

He studied his briefing notes on the way, Pete tended to prefer to speak "off cuff" but he had learned the hard way the importance of getting facts and figures correct. This morning he would meet senior members of the Saudi government who were in Barrow to seal a defence deal with the large employer there, British Aerospace. This would secure jobs for local people for the next five years and was a key part of his election pledge of Britain being a great place to invest. He would be joined by his Minister of Defence and other military leaders, this was indeed a big deal. The flight was now skirting with the Irish Sea with Liverpool just below as they started a descent in to Walney island. Walney Island aerodrome had been built during the second world war and although commercial flights had been attempted over the years it was now operated solely by British Aerospace and used only for flights to their operating bases and several other military locations. Coming in off the Irish Sea across Morecambe Bay it was never the easiest of landings with strong cross winds and visibility often low. Today however Pete had looked from the window making out his old hunting ground of Preston and Leyland in the distance then the tower at Blackpool and he was sure out of the other window he could see the Isle of Man in the distance. Shortly after, they were descending sharply down and landing expertly on the island and after disembarking he was in his second Range Rover of the day with Police Escort and within 10 minutes was walking into the British Aerospace property in Barrow in Furness. A secure room had been made available to the PM and his entourage and he was soon talking with the team about the important deal they were about to strike, checking protocols for the meeting before discussing the second part of the day after lunch.

After a short walk around the factory here at British Aerospace Barrow they would return to the plane for a short hop to a similar facility between Preston and Blackpool, from there he would complete an engagement at his old secondary school in Leyland prior to being driven up to Heysham where he and the Prince of Wales would jointly launch a green energy programme securing the future of more jobs in a community that frankly needed some good news right now.

The media had been well briefed and coupled with the news he was about to deliver in Barrow this was set to be one of the proudest days of his premiership creating job security and new roles for thousands of people in the region that he had grown up in.

The call in to his old comprehensive school in Leyland hadn't been included in the media briefing so his Range Rover, security detail and Police Escort made for quite a sight as they exited the M6 motorway at Leyland before crossing the town finding westfield drive and pulling in to Worden High School. He didn't recognise parts of Leyland with the market long gone and many of the factories belonging to the automotive industry also consigned to the history book. He had, however, recognised the names of local businesses and some of the pubs and other hang outs from his youth still survived and he had briefly been overwhelmed with nostalgia. The visit had been arranged by one of his MP's who had also attended the same school and was now representing the area of West Lancashire.

Incredibly their old English Teacher was still in her role but due to retire and he had agreed to visit both to talk to students about his journey to the role of PM and present a gift to one of the counties longest standing teachers. Externally the school hadn't changed too much nor had the surrounding streets and Pete had felt quite emotional on his approach with his mind flitting back to escapades with friends and the people who had influenced his life and in some cases continued to do so. Internally the school had modernised and looked far more professional than his time there but with such a short timescale on the premises he was whisked into the school hall and an assembly of the current cohort for who he gave a short speech before taking a wide range of questions about his time at the school and his journey to the top job in the country. As he took the last question he could see his private secretary motioning frantically from the side of the school hall stage, he brought the questions to a close and sought out his private secretary who quickly whispered a message into his ear. As he left the hall with his purposeful walk it didn't go unnoticed by the head of the school and a number of the teachers that Pete's smile had disappeared and he looked pale with shock, as he climbed back in to the car and leant back in his seat he knew that a piece of history that had dogged his life for years was about to explode in to the public domain.

Just 25 miles north of Pete's current position the Prince of Wales exited the train at Lancaster station, this was as far as they could go as their adapted train would not cope with the small branch line down to the port of Heysham. After greeting well-wishers mainly assembled from local schools the Prince and his consort had a short walkabout before entering the car that would take them down to Heysham. As they pulled away for the short drive to the coast the Prince shivered as if someone had stepped across his grave, something didn't feel right but he couldn't work out what it was that was troubling him. His consort realised something wasn't right and held his hand tightly then the penny dropped as to what had spooked him, it was almost the 25 year anniversary since the death of Diana, Princess of Wales, and memories flooded back of the day, his trip to Paris and the subsequent media frenzy. He leaned back in his seat somewhat relieved that he had solved the riddle of his angst and started to focus on the day ahead. He had only met the PM on a small number of occasions and had found him hard to connect with, clearly a deep thinker he had struggled to make inroads in to his thinking but he was keen to change this and felt that today would be an important joint approach if in the future if they were to build a positive relationship as King and PM.

The Prince was taking far more of the burden of Royal Appointments after the death of his father and the age of his mother who now spent most of her time in Scotland at Balmoral. However, this trip was his initiative with his passion for green energy and as he stepped out of the car before the media assembled at Heysham the smile was genuine and warm as he met the team from the power station for a short lunch and tour.

Chapter 31   The Irish Sea

The Silver Wind was progressing well on its journey across towards Glasson dock and the skipper eased off the power a little to save the old girl from straining too much. The crew of four had this crossing off to a tee normally and the skipper frowned as it was just after 10am and the regular cup of tea and morning bacon sandwich hadn't arrived at the normal time, "what could be keeping them" he thought. They were in a busy area with a lot of commercial traffic and a number of seagoing yachts enjoying the last of the late summer, if they had been in a quieter area he would definitely have gone and investigated where the guys were and why his morning brew hadn't appeared. He was certain he had heard movement below deck and a scraping or scratching noise of metal on metal but he couldn't be sure, however he was regretting not checking the hold to make sure everything was secure before leaving port this morning. The truth was that he had become so trusting and proud of his colleagues in this quiet port that he never felt the need to question their work. At that moment the door behind him opened and he was knocked to the floor and his head began to spin.

He was dragged back to his feet by four pairs of hands belonging to two men who to the skipper seemed barely out of their teens, his first question was "what have you done with my crew", he was pushed roughly and told to keep quiet. His next thought was these two men were not disguised in anyway, they clearly had no fear of being caught, then finally he randomly thought "they all need a good wash".

One of the men pushed the skipper in the back with what felt like something metallic and asked him aggressively to explain what he was seeing on the radar. The skipper described the various shipping he could see but they wanted to know why they couldn't see the new flagship ferry also coming across from the Isle of Man. He explained that it wouldn't have left the Island yet but if they maintained their current course and speed they would likely cross its plotted course in around 2.5 hours given the difference in speed of the respective vessels. They had left him in no doubt what would happen if he disobeyed orders and he was keen that the rest of the crew were not injured so he meekly followed their instructions though he had already told them three times that this small coaster was already operating at its maximum engine speed.

Though he had no idea what was going on he knew that he was in a dire position, there was no way of raising an alarm that wouldn't alert his captors but then glancing to his left and seeing the radar screen he saw something that lifted his spirits slightly.

The day before

Colin was walking back to the bus stop for the number 3 bus that would take him back to Douglas, in his hoody and cap he looked just like the majority of other locals or tourists making their way home at the end of this late summers day. He had spent the day observing the movements of Tanweer, Shazad and Hussain watching them eventually hide themselves away on the quay, this had been different from other days so he had called the number of his handler to explain what he had seen and was surprisingly told to stand down and await further instructions. As the bus dropped down and on to the promenade in Douglas he was still puzzled as to why the change in instructions and what was about to go down. Knowing he could relax slightly he walked the rest of way into Douglas and settled down in the Counting House pub with a pint of Okell's bitter and relaxed. He checked the options for travelling off the island the next morning but for some reason he wasn't able to book on any of the ferries over to the mainland so instead booked a one way ticket by plane to Liverpool, he wasn't just travelling back to mainland UK, he was going home at last.

The next morning as Colin headed up to the islands airport he saw the new island ferry in port and the activity around it as people busily prepared for its departure. It was mainly empty freight units he could see being loaded and on a weekday slightly off season passenger loadings would be relatively light. Colin noticed a new style Land Rover Defender pass him on the quay with a second almost identical vehicle behind, expensive vehicles were certainly not rare on the island but something about the way the two were travelling in convoy made him take note and he was certain he had seen the vehicles before as they disappeared through the port gates to the area reserved for vehicles and their passengers.

John had arrived early for his shift today, he would be taking over from the Master who had brought the vessel on its overnight sailing from Heysham and as they did a handover on the bridge there was little of note to report, the ship was handling well and things boded well for what was to be a momentous day he was sure. Still he had to do all his checks, speak to the engineering leads and front of house team before one final check of the weather and a last summary of the expected weight that was being loaded. A business lounge at the front of the ferry had been reserved for various dignitaries who would be travelling over for todays ceremonies and as soon as they were out of the harbour he intended to pass control to his second in command and be visible as a key member of the company that ran the ferries.

At the harbourside the two Land Rover Defenders drove on through the stern of the ship, there were no official border checks for what was classed as a domestic crossing with just a few random searches carried out and these mainly on incoming passengers not those travelling the other way. Dada got out of the drivers seat and headed up to check in on board and receive the cabin keys which they had booked for privacy even on such a short crossing of around 3 hours and 45 minutes. As soon as he had the cabin keys he text the cabin numbers to Chris and then they all left the Land Rover Defenders and went straight to the cabins where they quickly closed the doors behind them.

Chris was nervous but this was nothing compared to Adnan who he observed to look horrendous like he hadn't slept and so nervous he looked like he might throw up at any minute. Chris asked him if he was alright and Adnan replied that he wasn't looking forward to the crossing as he didn't have sea legs, a comment that Chris found odd he had never mentioned before, something didn't seem right.

John handed over control of the ship to his second in command and vacated his seat, it suddenly struck him how technology had changed and as he looked back as he left the bridge his second in command was deep in concentration sat in what looked like a huge gaming chair with a central console and joystick that controlled the ship – something akin to games consoles in the 1980's chuckled Chris to himself. He headed downstairs swiping his pass which recorded he was leaving the bridge area before heading down to have a brief discussion with the ships purser's before entering the business lounge. Chris was a tall handsome guy so naturally people looked at him when he entered the lounge, the uniform and insignia just adding to the sense of gravitas he brought wherever he went on board. The companies PR manager and CEO were on board and Chris discussed the rehearsal that was about to take place, he also confirmed that they were expecting an on time arrival and an easy crossing. He took an orange juice and did some networking round the lounge staring out over the bow of the ship and out to sea seeing nothing out of the ordinary

Chapter 32   London

The MI6 Building at Vauxhall Cross in London houses the headquarters of the Secret Intelligence Service (SIS), also known as Military Intelligence, Section 6 (MI6), the United Kingdom's foreign intelligence agency. It is located on Albert Embankment in Vauxhall, London, on the bank of the River Thames beside Vauxhall Bridge. The area had had previously been a no go area for most tourists with a mixture of run down pubs, sleazy massage parlours and a carbuncle of a transport interchange. But redevelopment was ripping through the area with sought after apartments surrounding the area, green space created and cultural icons such as Battersea Power Station just a short walk away. In the most secure of briefing rooms those assembled, including the deputy director general, were working unusually closely with their MI5 colleagues who primarily focussed on domestic issues. However, the case they were viewing in live feed in front of them had the ability to rock the countries reputation at home and abroad so a joint working party had assembled with lines open to every agency who may be able to support in this ongoing operation. In front of them was a video screen the size of a typical commercial cinema unit and on it the screen was split so they could see the ferry on the left hand side whilst on the right there was a zoomed out map of the Irish Sea monitoring both ship and air movements although to be on the safe side they had already enabled a no fly zone over the area which was causing significant logistical issues to the North Wests two international airports Manchester and Liverpool.

DCO Williamson was a veteran of many operations over his twenty year career and commanded respect when he asked those present to prepare for his briefing. He dealt with those on the small coaster Silver Wind first talking about the threat analysis, imminent danger and the background he had gathered. Thinking inwardly he had to be honest with himself and admit the three young adults aboard the ship, Shezhad, Tanweer and Hussain had puzzled him most. He had sent a team in to the Mosque in Leeds only to find that like many similar establishments in the City the Mosque was a beacon of hope rather than a beacon of hate and had won awards for its community cohesion, whilst they had recalled the group of young men it was clear this had simply been a regular booking of the adjacent community space and nothing to do with the mosque itself, payments for hire had been made in cash and there was no CCTV footage either from the building or local area that showed anything other than the young men meeting at the centre. Similarly the team that had simultaneously visited the outward bound centre in the Lake District had found a centre renowned for creating opportunities for troubled communities and the booking had been made via a PayPal address that had led them nowhere.

A small team had also visited Kenya and despite continued rumblings around repatriations after the countries past colonialism cooperation with the respective intelligence agencies had remained strong and they had received 100% support in-country and particularly the coastal resort of Mombassa but again the trail had quickly run cold, it had also been reported that a fourth young male had been working with Shezhad, Tanweer and Hussain but they had found no definite connection despite extensive investigations, similarly when they looked at the family history of the three young men the only thing they had in common was they came from good families, well educated with happy childhoods and nothing to suggest they would choose an extreme path in life. He then went on to talk about the Kahil family and their arrival on the Isle of man some 25 years ago, whilst he focussed on the current brain behind the business empire, Dada, he revealed previous investigations in to his father the disgraced businessman who was recently deceased, in the case of the latter though it appeared that all his dealings had been with pro British agencies and there had never ever been anything to suggest an anti UK angle indeed he had tried to ingratiate himself with every part of UK society. He then focussed on Dada and his life prior to arriving on the Isle of Man and of course "the accident" in Paris.

Prior to becoming world wide news in 1997 Dada had been a low profile figure and seen as most as a spoilt son of a billionaire, details of how he had survived the "accident" and his subsequent arrival on the Isle of Man remained a mystery to many in the intelligence community but it was known through limited intercepts that he had become extremely anti UK establishment, that said there had been nothing specific that had brought him to the attention of the security services. Williamson didn't like to deal on conjecture but was forced to conclude that the only motive he would have according to his background would really be revenge. After the accident in Paris he had been hunted by media and spooks alike and his only one comment to media when he had resurfaced some years later was he had no recollection of the accident, what had caused it, where he had been in the intervening period nor who was in the car with him.

Williamson then went on to talk about Dada's family, Dada was probably best known for his relationship with Diana Princess of Wales but DNA taken by the French Security Services at the time of the incident had proven that her body had been in the car. For the past 25 years there had been lots of suggested sightings of her both in the UK and around the world but mainly these had been reported in sensational news stories typical of the British press and it had been hard to give any of them credence.

Just as he was concluding his assessment he received a message from Royal Navy Command indicating they had a vessel within striking distance of the Silver Wind and had high confidence they could launch a raid on the vessel and capture it and its occupants without risk of detection. Williamson looked over at the deputy director general of MI5 who duly authorised the mission.

Back on board the Manxman Johns second in command put a radio call through to him asking him to return to the bridge. He knew this must be urgent as he knew he could be trusted so he made his excuses and walked purposefully without causing unnecessary panic. Up on the bridge his officer showed him the track of the Silver Wind, a much slower vessel that John was sure carried small cargo loads from the Island, it would have set sail hours before them but looking at its tracking history he could see that it would cross their path in around an hours time if they both maintained their current speed.

However, the reason he had been called back up the bridge was an hour previously it had suddenly changed course from a pretty direct route across to Glasson Dock to instead pass right in front of the Manxman ferry. Looking at the radar and tracking system they were both surprised to see another larger vessel behind the Silver Wind, coloured purple on the display this meant it was a Navy vessel. But what really perplexed them was as they stood staring at the screen together both vessels disappeared from the system like someone had turned the light off. John took his long range binoculars and went out on to the external area of the bridge on the port side, after scanning the area he expected to see the Silver Wind he indeed could see it and some distance behind the outline of the Navy Vessel, he thought maybe his eyes were deceiving him when he could see the a wake from what he presumed was a fast moving inflatable. He went back on to the bridge and asked his second in command to increase speed slightly and maintain the current course before heading down to alert the companies CEO.

As he headed back in to the public areas he saw a young man approaching from the opposite direction, he stared right through John who had to move out of his path to avoid a collision between the two, at that point he remembered where he had seen the face before, "something didn't feel right" thought John.

Back at MI5 HQ Williamson smiled a grim determined smile as the screen in front of them showed the special forces team board the silver wind, within 5 minutes they received a message from Navy HQ confirming that the vessel had been captured along with all of its occupants who had surrendered meekly without a fight. The three youths they had taken would now be airlifted to a secure location for immediate questioning, although a thorough search was still taking place, whatever the threat was from the Silver Wind it seemed to have been averted. The Deputy Director General was speaking to Downing Street to try and postpone the events later in the day but the PM's staff so far steadfastly refused to change plans and he would shortly be arriving in Heysham where the future King was already on walkabout.

Chapter 33   Morecambe Bay

A deck below the lounge on the ferry where John was being briefed by the dignitaries, Adnan was lying on his bed in the cabin when there was a knock at the door, through the spyhole he could see it was his father so he unlocked the door and let HIM in, but before he could say anything Dada started talking urgently with Adnan getting angrier and angrier with every word. It became clear that the mission with his three friends had all been a sham, a diversionary tactic to both confuse Adnan and hopefully steer the authorities away from what was really going to happen today. The trips to Leeds, Kenya and the Lake District as well as all the careful planning had all been manufactured by his father, or his fathers brother to be precise. As his mind raced he realised how stupid he had been, how they have never been challenged and his father had never questioned where he had been and who he was with. The anger was boiling up inside him and as the ship rocked slightly and his father stumbled, Adnan grabbed him by the neck and wrestled him to the floor. But Dada was strong, despite not being an outdoors person and a near recluse, years of daily work outs in the gym gave him upper body strength and he fought back hard. But ironically the training Adnan had gone through funded by Dada himself had toughened him into a young man and gradually he was winning the battle and eventually found himself astride his father. With his knee digging in to his fathers shoulders as he had been taught in the training, Dada was incapacitated and Adnan grabbed the wall mounted fire extinguisher crashing it down on his fathers head and with the sickening cracking of bone he realised he had landed a mortal blow.

Adnan stopped to tidy himself up and change his sweatshirt thinking incredibly logically before striding through to the stern of the ship. He passed through the bar area then the main customer lounge not even registering that he had nearly knocked the ships captain from his feet such was his desire to get to the outside deck. When he got there he scanned the sea but couldn't see the Silver Wind anywhere, connecting to the ships Wi-Fi he also scanned the maritime app on his phone and couldn't believe his eyes when the Silver Wind seemed to have completely disappeared from the radar too.

He realised the plan was over, there was no way he could complete the mission, the weaponry had all been with his three comrades on the Silver Wind. He stood looking out to sea and then realised whilst he might not be able to rock the establishment with force he could rock it with his brain and with the plan still formulating in his mind he headed back to the deck where his cabin was but instead of returning to his own room he banged aggressively on his mothers door. The door opened cautiously at first then fully and as it opened he was shocked to see Chris who quickly grabbed him and pulled him in to his mothers cabin.

Colin had flown back to Liverpool and with it being a short hop and a domestic flight, and only having a small case, he was soon out of the airport and striding across to the car hire desks less than an hour after leaving the Isle of Man. The message from Pete had come completely out of the blue but he knew deep down he could not ignore the request. He therefore hired a nondescript Ford Saloon and eased it out of the space and on to the motorway eventually joining the M6 motorway north towards Preston and then onwards to Lancaster. Just before the motorway exit for Lancaster is an art deco service station built not long after the road was opened and his instruction was to leave the vehicle on the southbound side so he exited at the Lancaster exit before rejoining the motorway south immediately exiting at the service station. He left the key for the vehicle on top of the drivers side front wheel, put on his sunglasses and headed over the motorway on the bridge before leaping a fence crossing fields on to the old A6 road where he waited for a bus south to Preston. Although he had not been asked to he sent an SMS text message to the number Pete had called from detailing where he had left the Ford and threw the phone he was using in to a local stream by the road side after switching it off as instructed. He was both thirsty, hungry and feeling dirty after spending the day travelling, tomorrow he was going to start reclaiming his empire but for tonight he went on-line and booked himself a room at the Holiday Inn in the centre of Preston, he was back and literally just yards from the territory he saw as his.

Around an hour later Pete was heading north on the same part of the M6 motorway Colin had been on earlier, the Range Rover had its tailing security detail as well as a member of his security team sat in the passenger seat. Normally he would work in the adapted rear seats taking on board briefings or calls from cabinet colleagues but right now he needed some thinking time. Minutes later they were just south of the service station and Pete demanded that the vehicle left the motorway citing the fact he was bursting for the washroom. Both the security officer and driver looked back at him nervously as this had not been part of their travel plan but Pete demanded they stop. After the security team had conferred and scanned the area Pete and the driver left the vehicle and headed into the service station, with his head down and purposeful walk be barely attracted a glance from the other road users. His driver positioned himself outside the Gents facilities not allowing anyone to enter, Pete knew once inside he had only around 2 minutes but luckily immediately spotted a fire door which he walked straight through and out in to a maintenance area behind, he threw his suit jacket in a waste bin putting on a denim jacket he saw hanging on a coat hook left no doubt by an employee of the service area. He walked quickly across the bridge spanning the motorway on to the south side of the service station and out in to the parking area, he immediately spotted the Ford, found the key and drove steadily so as not to attract attention, but instead of joining the motorway he headed out through a small service road normally used by emergency and maintenance vehicles then turning east and away from the motorway in to the Lancashire countryside towards Dolphinholme then Abbeystead and in to an area known as the Trough of Bowland.

Around five minutes later and back at MI5 HQ Williamson took a call and those around him noted the change in his complexion as he looked over to them saying "you're not going to believe this but we've lost the fucking prime minister". The deputy Director General replied "I can beat that son, we are about to implement operation Tower Bridge, Prince Charles will be leaving Heysham shortly for Balmoral, his mothers condition is deteriorating and she is not expected to see out the next 24 hours, based on what we know at the moment we have neither a functioning Prime Minister or Head of State and there is no guide book for what to do next, what do you suggest Williamson?".

At around the same time Colin had left the Ford at the service station near Lancaster Prince Charles private secretary had taken a call from Balmoral, at the earliest opportunity he took the Prince to one side and relayed the news about his mothers health, whilst it was not entirely unexpected the Prince looked visibly shocked before he composed himself and requested immediate transport to be scrambled, his private secretary explained he had already given that instruction to save time and the Prince would be driven to the helipad at the other side of the nuclear facility from where they expected to be at Balmoral within 90 minutes. His consort squeezed his hand in a rare show of public affection but he looked at her almost coldly and said "no, you must stay and complete the days appointments then join me in Scotland later" and within minutes he was in an RAF helicopter headed to Balmoral.

Pete was travelling deeper in to the Trough of Bowland but as remote as he knew the area was he knew he needed to lose the vehicle he was in quickly. He pulled in to a small service road to a reservoir used by the local utility company and walkers close to the hamlet of Abbeystead and parked in the small parking area where he changed in to the clothes and trainers Colin had left in the hire car for him as requested and put on the sunglasses, leaving the vehicle unlocked he crossed two fields and back on to the road he had driven on and headed towards the Abbesystead Estate which he reached within 10 minutes. He knew the estate well having worked for the gamekeeper "beating the grouse" in the 1980's then visiting the owner, the Duke of Westminster, when plotting to become PM. Abbeystead House was built in the 1880's and had long been a regular destination for politicians and royalty alike who came to enjoy the outdoors, hunting and exquisite food prepared by the staff, yet to almost all people outside of the little hamlet it was virtually unknown despite spreading across 18,000 acres. In the 1980's the Abbeystead Estate had been bought by the Duke of Westminster Gerald Grosvenor and Pete had last visited just before his sudden death only 6 years before. During the visit he had been totally off radar and they had enjoyed time shooting, walking and running but learned a lot about the estate, its facilities and equipment, this knowledge was about to come in handy.

Back on the Manxman ferry the reception who had gathered for the naming ceremony were enjoying the free drinks and canapes with conversation flowing and other than the few ferry company staff on the vessel most were oblivious to the fact the ferry had slowed down considerably as it started to approach Morecambe bay and the last leg of the journey in to the harbour at Heysham. Murmurs had started to circulate though that Prince Charles wouldn't be naming the ship due to the deteriorating health of his mother, the news coming via the on board rolling satellite news channels. John had just returned to the bridge realising there was an issue with the reduced speed and by his reckoning they were also several miles off course. By the time he reached the bridge of the ship he was feeling angry that his second in command hadn't contacted him but his anger calmed when he was told they had just been put in to a holding pattern by the Vessel Traffic Service (VTS) at Heysham due to a technical issue in the harbour. Realising everything was in hand he headed back down to the reception explaining to his second in command he expected to be informed the minute anything changed.

Meanwhile down in the cabin Chris was still computing the message he had received from his MI5 handler Williamson via satellite phone when Adnan had knocked on the door, the instruction had been clear to neutralise Adnan but now he found himself in the cabin with the boy and his mother. Adnans mother asked Adnan where his father was but he just smirked and said "you wont be seeing him again", "you mean he is dead, his mother said?" and Adnan just leant back and laughed, his eyes dancing crazily, it was only when he calmed down and looked again at his mother he realised that far from looking upset she had a satisfied smile on her face and at this point whilst distracted Chris pounced and held him in a vice like headlock, wrestled him on to bed and before he knew it his arms and feet were tied and his mouth gagged.

Back at Vauxhall Cross the team were stretched to their maximum with the start of Operation Tower Bridge relating to the potential death of the Queen and the fact the PM was missing, there had never been a constitutional situation such as this before in the countries long history. Somehow Williamson was managing to stay calm and as he briefed those present confirmation came through that Chris who was operating for them on the ferry had control of Adnan, although he had refused to neutralise him, and a potential serious terrorist incident was now under control. The Palace had called twice in the last 30 minutes wanting to understand the situation with the ferry as the Princes consort, Camilla, was still at Heysham and would carry out the naming ceremony in her husbands absence. The assembled group made the decision to remove Adnan from the ship and insert the Marines as additional security and Chris was instructed to move Adnan to the top deck and the helipad area as soon and as discretely as possible but using any force necessary if he absolutely had to. Back on the ferry Chris turned Adnan over surprisingly gently and made him stand up removing his gag before saying to him "is there anything you would like to say to your mother before we leave" then before he could answer in a quiet but firm voice she said "Chris you know full well that Adnan is not my son", before anyone else could speak Chris gagged Adnan again and moved him in to the corridor and towards the rear staircase of the ferry and Adnan could feel the cold mouth of a pistol pointing in to his back.

Chapter 34   Morecambe Bay and Lancashire

Just a few miles north of the Manxman ferry at the MOD airfield on Walney Island the Merlin MK4 had landed around an hour before and was being refuelled and ready for flight again. The 12 marines boarded and their commander looking round the cabin realised that although the helicopter could carry almost double this amount of people it was important they had capacity as the day was so far advancing at a fast pace. He had some of the best men available in the cabin with him, people he would trust his life with and people he needed to be able to stay quiet about the national incidents that were unfolding in front of them.
They closed the door to the Merlin and the rotors started and within 2 minutes they were rising before turning and heading south across Morecambe Bay and towards the Manxman ferry where half the occupants in the cabin were to extract from the helicopter and ensure the Manxman was secure and no one could board the ferry. The ferry soon came in to view and they swooped in low just a few metres above its wake before rising slightly and in a text book display of flying hovered above the deck whilst one half of his team disembarked and the other half made short work of lifting Chris and Adnan in to the Merlin Helicopter and securing them in the cabin before rising and heading west back towards the Isle of Man. All this had been achieved in less than 10 minutes and with the stealth

equipment on the Merlin machine it had been achieved without anyone on board the ferry realising what had happened.

From the flight deck of the helicopter the Silver Wind soon came in to view and in another text book exercise the marines winched themselves down with Chris and Adnan securing them in the wheelhouse of the small cargo carrier before extracting themselves and returning to Walney Island. It hadn't gone unnoticed by Chris that two of the crew had disappeared to another area of the vessel before leaving the small ship and he quickly tried to run options through his head and try and understand what was happening around him.

Douglas Isle of Man

Despite advice to the contrary Aimee was again taking a walk along the promenade in Douglas and had already covered a mile when she felt she needed to rest. Towards the southern end of the promenade and close to the ferry terminal is a sculpture of the famous Bee Gees band commemorating their links to the island and she knew if she made it there she would be able to sit on the benches close by. As she sat down she realised she was overcome with sickness, not relating to her pregnancy but a pain that ran through her body that told her without any logic that something in her world was feeling very wrong, she didn't know where Chris was or when he would be back but suddenly somehow she knew that he was in some sort of serious danger.

Some 40 miles from where Aimee sat the Silver Wind was still anchored and rocking quite gently in the relatively calm weather conditions. Chris had been in and around military circles all his life and was wise enough to know what was about to happen, he looked across at Adnan who looked like a frightened toddler and despite having his gag removed by the marines had said nothing. But he raised his head and looked across at Chris with hate in his eyes and asked "when we were in the cabin on the ferry why didn't you kill me?". Chris paused before answering causing great effect whilst not meaning to and replied "because you are my son Adnan". They were the last words either of them heard as a huge explosion ripped through the small ship destroying it and its occupants instantly.

On the promenade at Douglas Aimee saw a dog being walked by its owner suddenly turn its head, prick up its ears and look out to sea then an instant later like many island residents Aimee heard a loud explosion and subsequent echo's reverberate around the bay, the feeling of sickness overwhelmed her and she leaned forward and vomited.

John was called back to the bridge of the ship by his second in command and to his shock saw that the entrance to the bridge was guarded by two people in fatigues and holding what to John looked like automatic machine guns. Suddenly the door to the bridge opened and the commanding officer of the marines ushered him in. He immediately remonstrated about the intrusion and how he was in command of the ship but was told curtly, "when I'm on your ship or indeed any ship, I'm in command.

Opening a laptop the commanding officer linked in the team led by Williamson at MI5 HQ, Williamson was curt and to the point as he explained to john that the commanding officer of the small Marines force was now in command of the ship and he should follow all instructions for the safety of all aboard, he was to personally take control of the ship on its final approach in to Heysham but react to any instructions he was given. John was used to giving orders but realised he had no choice in this matter although he went on to ask what was the threat to the vessel. Williamson said they were certain all threats to the vessel had been eliminated but they were still securing the shore and harbour area but fully intended to go ahead with the Royal Visit and naming ceremony, John explained that he understood whilst at the same time knowing something on board was just not right.

Chapter 35   Around Central Lancashire

Pete climbed in to the old Landrover Defender in the garages at the edge of the estate, it fired up first time and he slowly eased it out and on to the lane to the main road, he realised he looked slightly ridiculous in what he was wearing so he put on a hunting jacket he found in the back along with a hunting cap and headed across the Trough of Bowland where he joined the A6 driving down towards Preston. The streets looked as normal as usual with people going about their business, he had put the radio on but the only major news item so far was that Prince Charles was on his way to Balmoral as his mothers health seemed to be deteriorating. In his position Pete knew what this meant in reality, Charles would almost certainly be travelling after receiving a call indicating his mother, The Queen, was close to passing away. But Pete's mind wasn't really on the news as he was thinking about where he could abandon the land rover without leaving himself a long walk. He had to balance this however with the possibility of discovery and he knew it would only be a matter of time before the Landrover was reported missing then linked to him and traced to his location. He skirted around Preston then picked up a smaller road that took him through the suburbs and on to the West of Leyland where his parents lived. There was still nothing on the radio news stations about his disappearance and his considered opinion was nothing would be released until the

Security Services had a working hypothesis of what was happening but he knew his family may be watched both digitally and physically, he knew he may have only minutes, possibly hours so he pulled in to the car park of a busy garden centre and farm shop on the road towards Southport before heading across country to his parents house.

Their house was pretty much as it was when he had left home 35 years previously, a typical suburban semi with kids playing in the street and cars and delivery vans coming and going frequently. He went to the rear of the property and entered through the back door which his parents always left open when they were at home, as he entered the kitchen his Mum turned round and gasped and dropped the pan she was holding burning her feet with boiling water in the process. "Pete" she mouthed quietly at him before he filled the silence by explaining this was a flying visit and he would be gone in less than 30 minutes. His mother made him a string cup of tea and toast smothered in butter which he devoured as they talked quickly. She knew something was very wrong, even though she led a relatively sheltered life she knew that PM's don't suddenly go off grid and appear at their parent's house, her first question was the motherly instinct of "are you in trouble", but despite his position and his age he couldn't bring himself to tell his mother what the issue was so he simply smiled and went upstairs to his room which was as it had been left when he moved out all those years ago and probably untouched since he was in the room a year previously on a family visit. He reached into one of the clothes drawer and pulled out the pay as you go handset that he hadn't used for several years. To his surprise it fired into life and he quickly typed out a message "I always said that money was jinxed, its all yours now, good luck, Pete". He changed into some old clothes pulled on a baseball cap and went back downstairs, he gently held his Mum and said "thank you, love you" before leaving by the same door and walking at pace down the street and towards Leyland.

His Mother knew something wasn't right but knew she had to let him go, she watched him walk down the street until she could no longer see him then sat down at her kitchen table and put her head in her hands and cried. Pete walked through the park where he had played as a child dropping the phone he had used into the bin before carrying on past his secondary school, through the woods and out on to the main shopping street. Whilst many of the names from his childhood had gone he still recognised the properties, the old cinema, the old post office and his favourite bakers by the roundabout. He walked purposefully nodding politely at anyone who passed him but ultimately fixed on the road ahead. Eventually he arrived at a small play area via a blue bridge over the main west coast railway line where he stood and leaned on a fence looking back across at Leyland his home town, it had been a long day yet it was only just before five to two in the afternoon.

He heard the iron railway lines start to tingle which indicated the approach of a train, he leaped the fence and stood by the side of the track as the Glasgow to London train approached, the train had left Preston just 5 minutes earlier and was almost at its cruising speed of 100mph when the driver saw Pete by the side of the track, he blew the horn frantically knowing that at this speed it would take the train around half a mile to stop even if he applied the brakes but he saw the figure take off his jacket and cap and step on to the line in front of him, he applied the brakes knowing he couldn't stop and just before the point of impact he looked in to the mans eyes and was certain he mouthed "sorry" at him. As a career train driver he knew the process he had to follow and also knew there would be nothing that could be done to save the man but he immediately called the emergency services and his control centre before recording in his operating book the time of impact, it was five to two.

His Mum looked out of the kitchen window and saw the unmarked car pull up outside her house, the doors opened and two non uniformed officers came straight to the house pushing open the front door shouting "where is he, where is he". With tears rolling down her cheeks she looked at them each in turn before saying "he's gone, Pete is long gone."

On board the Manxman the assembled dignitaries were briefed by the ferry companies CEO who himself had just been briefed on the bridge by the Commanding Officer of the Marines. He told them everything that he knew which was there had been some security concerns that had been dealt with and the naming ceremony would go ahead but on the opposite side of the harbour, they were also made aware that Prince Charles was end route to Balmoral but that his wife would complete the engagement first coming on board to meet those assembled.

Down below in her cabin she was applying make up, after 25 years of living out of the public eye she had lost none of her beauty and style. She had chosen her outfit carefully and she patted herself down and grinned shyly at the full length mirror. The hat she put on reminded her of one she had seen the singer Michael Jackson wear almost thirty years ago, in fact she had remarked on his headwear when they had met in London. Finally she put on a pair of carefully chosen polarized glasses, the colour and large frame concealed not only her eyes but also part of her face but as she looked in the mirror she was happy with what she saw staring back at her.

The Duchess of Cornwall, Camilla, had grown frustrated at the delayed arrival of the ferry and she was desperate to be at her husbands side as soon as she could get to Balmoral, eventually one of his aides had said they were ready to go and they were taken by Range Rover round to the ferry which had just unloaded its main freight, car and foot passengers. They were met by the Kings Isle of Man representative, the Lieutenant Governor on the car deck and after small talk were taken by lift directly to the lounge containing all the dignitaries. The Prince had been briefed in the morning prior to is unscheduled departure but in the time they had been waiting for the ferry she had tried to memorise the key people she was to speak to and some facts about the islands flagship brand new lifeline ferry.

As she entered the room the noise abated as people turned to stare, something she was well used to, and she smiled inwardly that those gathered had clearly not held back on drinks during the delay with the smell of alcohol in the air. She was worked round the room by the lieutenant and the islands chief minister firstly meeting with legislative responsibilities on the island, she made various promises to visit and concentrated on not making errors about the islands status as part of the British Isles but not the United Kingdom.

Next she handed out recognition to those responsible for the design of the new ship and its safe transport from the shipyard where it was built in Asia before then starting to mingle with others in the room. She was not a drinker normally when on duty but after the day they had had she accepted a red wine from one of the ministers as she circled the room. She looked discretely at her wrist watch knowing she would be leaving the ship by 2.30pm, she was slightly mortified to see it was still only five to two. With her back to the entrance, she was looking out over the side of the vessel whilst one of the dignitaries bored her senseless on the statistics of the ship, she didn't hear or see the door open nor did she see anyone enter the room. Many of those gathered did see the door open though and many were captivated by the height, elegant and poise of the lady who entered the room. She walked purposefully but slowly directly towards Camilla who turned to see what was causing the commotion in the room, just then the woman took off her hat and glasses and looked directly at Camilla saying "I think the last time was in the drawing room at Sandringham wasn't it darling, how is my husband?" Camilla felt like the room was spinning and she dropped the wine glass as she realising she was looking straight in to the eyes of Diana, Princess of Wales.

That evening

For anyone aged 80 and under the Queen had pretty much been the only head of estate they could remember, her portrait had adorned bank notes, coins and stamps for generations and despite kickbacks about the UK's colonial past she was loved as much if not more through the old empire as she was in the UK. She had been there at the end of the second world war, the cold war and every post war significant event, her televised Christmas addresses were watched by millions every year. Her death brought the country to a standstill, events were cancelled and the main TV channels scrapped their schedules to bring news of her passing, tributes began to pour in from world leaders and it wasn't long before media outlets began to ask questions about the silence from Downing Street, in fact many commented on the irony of how the death of Diana had been a PR masterclass from the then PM whilst the Queen had come in for intense criticism, now the current PM was receiving criticism for his invisibility on the night a nation lost its mother figure.

Many other stories were starting to circulate on social media but the UK press agencies had received reporting restrictions instigated by the security services and were being prevented on commenting, however these stories started to grow legs and it had only been a matter of time as to when a foreign media channel published pictures and commentary on unfolding events in the UK.

At MI5 headquarters Williamson leaned back in his wheelchair and breathed out as if releasing months of pressure. The safe docking of the Manxman ferry in Heysham had been a relief and an operation that could receive no media coverage, or not in their lifetimes anyway. They had watched by camera in awe as Diana Princess of Wales had appeared in the lounge and caught the face of Camilla as the glass she was holding had fallen to the floor, this part of the plan had gone exactly as planned.

Formal identification was underway of the body found on the railway tracks at Leyland but CCTV cameras and a DNA test had confirmed what they already knew anyway. The country had lost a Queen and a PM but found the peoples Princess. The deputy Director General leaned across and shook Williamson by the hand before saying "well done Dave, I knew from the moment we picked you up from the Shetlands that you would be an asset".

Just outside Cairo an old man was watching the international news on Al Jazeera, images and names that appeared on the screen pricked his brain to life and back into another age. His wife had long since passed away and he lived with his daughter, herself still suffering from the injuries received in that awful car accident 25 years previously. He woke her excitedly saying "Mariam quick, come and see the news". Much of the news centred around the death of the Queen who had passed away peacefully earlier that evening but in another developing story media were starting to report the death of Dada Kahil and a picture of two men believed to have been involved in his death were flashed on the screen. Mariam almost missed the image and had to wind back and after she did the blood drained out of her face and she cried "No No, it cant be, that's Adnan, my son".

Postscript   December 2022 Preston Lancashire

Three months later Colin was sat in his office as the busy Christmas season was in full swing. Though nothing much phased him the last 3 months had seen revelation after revelation, the text and attachment from Pete had been mind blowing in its own right, not only had it been the last time he heard from Pete but the attachment contained information that could take down much of the previous and present establishment and, possibly, lead to the abdication of King Charles whose coronation had not yet even happened. Tomorrow he had an appointment with a media consultant who he had contacted last week, he was hoping the sale of the story and subsequent film rights would make him rich beyond belief.

He thought of the meeting almost 35 years ago with the group that had threatened to kill him if he didn't pass them intimate details about the bank in Preston, it was at this time he had realised he was a strong negotiator and despite his poor performance at school the opportunity to see an opening for himself had paid dividends. The group had a long term aim to reform the UK, banish the Royal family and install military type leadership, Pete had been in their pocket all through his career but his final acts had ensured that Colin would be seen as a good guy in it all and whilst he had cooperated with them throughout, he had secretly been feeding enough information to their old friend Dave to ensure their plan would not come to fruition.

He was brought back to earth when the alarm sounded as the rear exit alarm activated, the alarm and push bar had been fitted to stop customers using the emergency exit as a short cut through to the back alley and taxi rank, but in reality it hadn't reduced the route being used. He walked through to the back and saw the door hanging open and beyond that a wheelchair with its occupant smiling thinly at him, suddenly he heard a noise to his right and then a blow to the head as he was pulled into his own office. The last thing Colin remembered seeing was the room starting to spin and then a familiar voice said "did you really think we would let you live?" then a pause before the voice followed up with "and then there were two" then a prick to his arm then darkness.

December 2022 Dubai

Trudy walked down the boardwalk in Al Seef next to the creek river just a short walk from the rented apartment they had made home, she was excited to be meeting Aimee although the events of the last few months had made her nervous when out in public. This was a different part of Dubai away from all the glass buildings and plush malls, in the souk there were a mix of Turks and residents from the middle east selling a mixture of fine materials, spices and tourist trinkets. As she walked through the souk in the late afternoon heat she attracted a lot of attention pushing her pram with the shop keepers all shouting for her attention hoping she would enter their small shops. But she kept going until she reached the Costa Coffee shop by the river, partly relieved for the air conditioning yet mortified she hadn't been able to suggest somewhere more authentic to Aimee. Although they had been here a month she hadn't ventured out too much on her own and John was already training for his new career on the Mein Schiff German liners that plied their trade around the Arabian seas. After the events of summer John had felt he had been partly blamed for what happened on the ferry on that fateful day and they had been hounded by the media so it had been a pretty easy decision to make the move.

Unbeknown to Trudy, Dave had been sat in the very same coffee shop just before a meeting on behalf of the UK secret services with Mossad and the Signals Intelligence Agency (SIA), the latter being tasked with ensuring the security and integrity of the United Arab Emirates. The meeting had taken place on a nondescript transport ship called Al Shindaga moored in the creek outside one of the palaces of His Highness, the ruler of Dubai.

The SIA had been incredibly open about their relationship with the Kahil family and Al Kahil himself. Initially years ago the mission had been to infiltrate the

UK at the highest level as the UK had sought to block the growth of Dubai worried about its own place in the ever changing world. The predecessor of the SIA had bankrolled an operation to discredit or compromise well known figures from politics and had carried out a series of events (of which the bank robbery in Preston was one) which it had then pinned against people forcing their removal from public life, sometimes these people had been directly involved and sometimes not.

Al Kahil had been a key part of the plan and he had been tasked with infiltrating both the Royal Family and senior politicians but the plan had started to fail when rumours of his personal life, sexual misdemeanours and financial fraud had begun to circulate. The events in Paris 25 years before had been a convenient accident in bringing the plan to a close and ultimately Dubai had been more than standing on its own two feet and had nothing to fear from British interference in its affairs. Things had remained quiet until they had discovered Dada Kahil planned to launch himself into the top of UK society with Princess Diana who most people thought to have died in the Paris accident. The SIA could not let the truth come out, nor could the UK Government and along with Mossad who had infiltrated the Kahil family, an intricate operation was launched to ensure all loose ends were tied up and none of this ever reached the public eye. Al Kahil himself had been disgraced when news of his behaviour had reached the savage UK tabloid media and his reputation and business empire were ruined for ever.

For 25 years the world had considered the peoples princess had died in the Paris car crash even though conspiracy theories had abounded, in fact on this occasion the conspiracy theorists had been right. So far the UK government had kept her quiet and she was slowly integrating back in to society, as the mother of the first in line to the throne and clearly with a story to tell her every move was closely monitored and she had appeared all over traditional and social media even more often than those heady days of the 1990's.

Although he kept quiet, Dave knew that if she broke silence it would create another constitutional nightmare and if they silenced her it would create an equally difficult situation for the Government to deal with.

The meeting was cordial but at the end the representative of the SIA was clear, the UK had to mop up details at their end, no one who knew the full story could be left to tell that story, loose ends needed to be tied up and this order came from His Highness Sheikh Mohammed himself. Dave left the meeting feeling the heat literally and metaphorically and as he returned to the Canopy Hilton Hotel by the creek he sat and bought himself some thinking time before calling in to his boss in Vauxhall London.

Trudy saw Aimee pushing the pram towards the coffee shop and had a warm feeling in her heart as she thought of the times they had spent together as excited expectant mothers, Trudy waved to her then made room so she could sit comfortably with the pram out of the late morning sun which was burning today. It had been almost two months since they had seen each other in Douglas, the call had been a surprise when Aimee said she was travelling to Dubai but Trudy had understood that with Chris gone and the glare of publicity there would be little to hold Aimee in the Isle of Man.

After swapping news and with both babies asleep the chat went back to those fateful days of August and the immediate aftermath, as well as feeling there was nothing for her on the Isle of Man Aimee expressed her frustration at becoming homeless as the Kahil properties were seized by Government officials. It was also clear to Trudy that Aimee was torn between the pain of losing Chris and the fact that he had kept so much secret from her for so many years. Meeting Chris's family hadn't helped much as they too had been oblivious to everything that happened or was happening in his life, their summary seemed to be they didn't believe that such a quiet focussed person could possibly have been involved in the biggest news story of the 21st century.

Despite all that, Trudy could see that Aimee was picking up the pieces and was heading back to Africa for now, closer to family and far away from the trauma of this year. What had surprised Trudy was her being so adamant she wanted to tell the whole story of the Kahil family and all the events that had led to the explosive ending in August 2022, "this is the biggest opportunity of my life to make my millions, and it will set Chris Junior up for life" Aimee had told Trudy. Trudy had winced inwardly and said "Aimee, you are one of the very few people who knows the full story, what you know about events is not your biggest opportunity, it's your biggest risk".

As Aimee pushed the pram back down the boardwalk by the Creek river in the midday heat she could see the Hilton hotel in front of her, the words Trudy had said kept going round in her mind and she just wanted to get back to the privacy of her room and scream. Along the boardwalk locals selling ice cream, pop corn and drinks shouted towards her but she heard none of them, neither did she hear people offering her boat rides or other opportunities to see Dubai. As she approached the hotel she could feel her eyes welling up and tears rolled down her face and the most anxious feeling she had ever felt in her life. Despite the sun, the heat and the relative open space she was in, she suddenly felt cold and like she was dropping in to a dark hole. She also didn't see the dark Sedan parked outside the hotel, specially adapted for wheelchair access it didn't particularly stand out alongside all the other expensive cars apart from its diplomatic plates. As she walked past the vehicle the window lowered and the occupant stared after her before speaking discretely into his radio "That's her, that's the one we need to bring in". The Sedan pulled away slowly, Dave closed the window and leaned back in his seat, his job was done, he was going home.

Meet the author

A proud Lancastrian now living in the Yorkshire Dales, Ian started his writing career with the successful tailsinthedales series set in the Washburn valley close to Harrogate aimed at a junior audience featuring Charlie the dog and his farm friends.

His writing style generally fuses together real events with his love of travel, the outdoors and geopolitical events.

Ian is passionate about encouraging children to read or be read to and has commendations for his work in schools at home and abroad.

As well as writing Ian also appears at school events, rural markets & educational events promoting children's literature as well as ghost writing short stories and poetry for others.

Away from writing his passions are walking, running, live music and most sports.